50p

NURSE ON

CW00405009

Student Nurse Anne Pentrose came to England to make a new life for herself. But was nursing too drastic a change of career? The remorselessly attractive Dr Charles Farne certainly seemed to think that Anne should have stayed in Australia!

Books you will enjoy
in our Doctor Nurse series

NURSE ON LIVINGSTONE WARD

BY
JANET FERGUSON

MILLS & BOON LIMITED
15–16 BROOK'S MEWS
LONDON W1A 1DR

First published as a serial in Great Britain 1985 by Woman's Weekly

This edition published 1985 by Mills & Boon Limited, 15–16 Brook's Mews London W1A 1DR

© Janet Ferguson 1985

Australian copyright 1985 Philippine copyright 1985

ISBN 0 263 75236 4

Set in 10 on 11½ pt Linotron Times
03–1185–52,700

Photoset by Rowland Phototypesetting Limited Bury St Edmunds, Suffolk Made and printed in Great Britain by Richard Clay (The Chaucer Press) Limited Bungay, Suffolk

CHAPTER ONE

THE two young women slammed the door of the Nurses' Home, and stepped down into the busy street. It was nearly November—a grey, bleak, sheened-with-rain kind of day. It was Sunday morning, and the sound of bells from a dozen City churches tangled the air from Fleet Street to Bishopsgate.

'When will you pay me, say the bells of Old Bailey; when I grow rich, say the bells of Shoreditch.'

The words of the old childhood song rang through Anne's head, as she skirted a puddle and, like her friend Pru, clapped a quick hand to her cap. Both girls were in uniform, and their caps bore a single stripe. They were student nurses (learner nurses), they were on their way to the hospital, going on ward duty for the first time. The hospital was the Walbrook, one of the oldest in London. It was grey and looming and fortress-like, it occupied part of two streets; from its easterly windows the dome of St Paul's could be seen.

They had just completed their nine weeks on Introductory Block, another name for preliminary training, to prepare them for this day, this great day of going on to the wards. They had adjacent rooms in the Nurses' Home, and had hoped to share a ward, to be on ward duty together, but this wasn't to be the case. Anne had been allocated to Livingstone Ward, which was Male Medical, Pru to Female Geriatrics, and she moaned about this now: 'I thought they always put learners on in twos.'

'Well, obviously they don't,' Anne said, winding her

5

arms in her cape. It was warm, navy blue and scarlet-lined. 'What I would have liked more than anything else is another session in Block. I still feel very lacking in knowhow, and the thought of all those patients, *real* ones, scares me rigid, Pru.'

'You don't look scared, you never do,' Pru cast an envious glance at the calm set of her friend's features, at her wheat-gold hair parting in glossy wings beneath her cap. 'You look as though you could cope with anything, you look like a senior nurse.'

'That's because I'm three years older than you, and as for the confident look, it's one I've been trying to cultivate, I've practised in front of the glass!' Anne said this in a joking way, feeling as she did so a jab of misery that went too deep for words. She ignored the feeling, or tried to, and smiled back at her friend. 'Don't worry, Pru, we'll both survive and so, with luck, will the patients!' Pru lapsed into giggles, and the awkward moment passed.

It was ten a.m., an unusual hour for nurses to go on duty, but the time had been fixed by their clinical teacher, who had wanted to wish them well. 'After today,' she had told them, 'your time will be eight a.m. sharp, unless you're on the one o'clock shift, called "lates".'

They crossed over to Beyton Wing, and the glass doors opened for them—a large vertical mouth to swallow them up. Instantly the muted sounds of the hospital engulfed them, it was like being cocooned in a different world. The medical wards were on the fourth level, geriatrics on the first. Pru elected to walk up, and as Anne stepped to the lifts she caught a glimpse of her friend's stout figure plodding steadily upwards. There was a lagging, resigned reluctance about it, and she thought how true was the saying that it is sometimes better to travel than to arrive.

But there was nothing lagging about the lift, it fairly shot her upwards. She was no sooner in it than out again, standing on level four. There was polished parquet beneath her feet, while through the rain-speckled windows she could see the tops of the trees in the main courtyard.

The corridor to the left of the stairs had 'Livingstone' over its top. So this is it, she thought . . . Livingstone, here I come! She pushed at the doors and found herself in a long, wide passage, more like a busy street or thoroughfare. She set off down it, walking swiftly; there were doors on either side. Nurses were whisking in and out, one or two turned to stare. She heard the sound of water running, she smelled milk heating up, she glimpsed trolleys, and wheelchairs, and patients in dressing-gowns. The hospital chaplain, in his rustling black cassock, passed her, making a draught. And still the passage went on . . . and on . . . and on.

Sister Heyhoe's office was right at the end, just outside the ward. Anne was just about to tap on her door when she saw it was ajar. There were people talking inside the room, and she stayed her hand in mid-air; she had better not knock, it was better, perhaps, to wait. There was a bench seat against the wall, and she sat down on that, drawing her apron corners into her lap. From here she could see through into the ward, which spread out on either side. She could see charts clipped to the ends of the beds, she could see an infusion set, the rounded hump of a bed-cradle, and rows of pale green curtains to screen beds off for a measure of privacy.

A nurse walked down the centre aisle, pushing a metal trolley; mid-morning milky drinks were being served. It seemed a very long time to Anne since she and Pru had eaten. She didn't feel hungry so much as empty, and due to nervousness her inside was making noises like a sink. Even so, she could still hear the voices in the room. The female one was Sister's; Anne had met her last week at the School. Sister had called for an allocations list. The other voice was male and deep, yet it had a carrying quality. With a ping of shock she heard her own name; they were talking about her. She kept on listening, she couldn't help herself.

'Yes, Doctor . . . Anne Pentrose, and she's twenty-one, older than our usual first-year student . . .' And that, of course, was Sister. The man answered, sounding a little annoyed.

'Older or not, she's still inexperienced, she won't be much help for some time. You've had your whack of learners, they *always* seem to be here.'

'I need help at all levels, Doctor, and teaching has to go on. The Pentrose girl struck me as being keen and intelligent. She has about her an air of assurance, or perhaps I mean *re*assurance. She'll be good for the patients, excellent for their morale.' There was a muffled assenting sound from the man, then Sister carried on: 'She's from Australia . . . Melbourne, I think, or from that area. How I envy these girls their enterprise, their courage to uproot, and come right across the world to . . .'

'*Where* did you say she's from?'

'Australia.'

'God Almighty!' he sounded scandalised.

'It happens!' Sister tried a laugh.

'I know full well it happens! I know *too* right it does!' his laugh was the scathing kind. 'Do you mean to tell me she's been accepted into our Nursing School, that we've undertaken to train her as a state registered nurse, only to have her take herself back to the Southern Hemisphere at the end of three and a quarter years . . . well, I think that's typical!'

'The Director of Nursing tells me that she's here on a permanent basis.'

'I'll believe that if and when she proves it.'

Anne took off her cape and stood up. The man's sweeping statements rankled, but not really all that much. She had made her plans at the end of March, she had thought them out with care, using what judgment she could muster, but also being guided by the special help that comes in terrible times.

Her knock on the door sounded good and loud, it flapped open at once . . . so suddenly that she bent forward and nearly fell in. She straightened up, and smiled stiffly at the two people standing there – at the tall man, and at Sister who was short. The man's stare engaged hers. He was very well turned out—immaculate in his long white coat that hung down straight as a wall. His tie was navy, his shirt pale blue, his face strong-boned and gaunt, his hair reddish-brown, the crisply curling sort. Even in that quick-flash moment Anne felt sure he hated his hair. He would have liked it straight to match the rest of him.

Sister stepped forward, covering his front. She was short and plump and pink. Her cap sat erect on her jet black hair like a pile of stiff meringue. Anne stared at it in fascination. How did she keep it on . . . by remote control? No grips were visible.

'Come in, Nurse,' she smiled at Anne, moving away from the man. 'Dr Farne,' she looked up at him, 'meet Learner Nurse Pentrose. Nurse, this is Dr Farne, our Registrar.'

'Good morning,' he nodded at Anne, but he didn't add the word 'Nurse'. His arms were bent round a pile of folders, but even had they been free, she was fairly certain he wouldn't have offered his hand. There was a wide unspannable chasm between nurses and Registrars. Why, only last week she had read in one of her nursing magazines that a first-year nurse was the lowest form of life on the ward! So forget that at your peril, she cautioned herself.

'Doctor's just going,' said Sister, looking at the door, but the hint had no effect on him, he stood there hitching his folders, and staring at Anne in an on-and-off kind of way.

'Sister tells me you're from Australia.' He set his feet slightly apart.

'Yes, I came over here in the spring, to my grand-mother in Herts.'

'You'll find our ways and climate a drastic change from yours.'

His usage of 'our' and 'yours' was deliberate; the emphasis was plain. Anne flashed a retort, forgetting who he was. 'I was born in Hampstead, London,' she said, 'I remember it very well. I was nine when we all emigrated, when we left here as a family. My father and I came home twice on visits, so I know all about the climate. I even like it—I enjoy the cold and rain.'

'That sounds like bravado,' Charles Farne said, his face devoid of expression. One of his legs – long and narrow – scissored itself to the door. 'And if you run out of enjoyment you'll go back there, I expect . . . back to the land of the sun, and all the rest of it?'

'I expect so, yes,' she told him, smiling, but lying in her teeth, for she had no intention of ever going back. Home is where the heart is . . . the truest saying of all. Her home had been sold and her parents were dead. She would never see them again. She would never, ever, see them again, and the searing knowledge of that was always with her, yet was scarcely believable. She realised, of course, that Dr Farne knew nothing of her history, but nevertheless, in that pain-jarred moment, she felt she hated him. Anger flared, her fingers curled in her palms. 'Whatever happens,' she declared over-loudly, 'I intend to be fair to everyone. I shan't waste Government money, I know what it costs to train . . . to train a nurse, I went into it thoroughly.'

'I'm glad to hear it.' His voice was cool, he looked over her head at Sister. 'I'll be in my room for the next half-hour, going through this lot,' he said. He wedged the folders down with his chin and flicked open the door. 'Perhaps you'd give me a ring as soon as the ulcer case arrives. The ambulance picked him up at ten, he's coming from Old Haverton. Why not allocate his ad-mission to Nurse Pentrose?' His eyes swung to Anne again. 'She could assess him and try her hand at a care-plan, under supervision, of course. There's nothing like plunging them in at the deep end, it's the quickest way to learn.'

Sister said something like, 'We'll see,' but the snap-ping shut of the door drowned her words. She sat down at her desk. 'I see you know how to defend yourself, Nurse, but don't overdo it,' she warned. 'Dr Farne is adept at turning the tables, it doesn't do to be pert.' Then without a pause, and giving Anne no chance at all to reply, she began to explain the working of the ward. 'Remember, you'll be putting into practice what you've learned in Block so far. In other words, you'll be learn-ing by *doing*, which is what nurse-training means. And don't worry, it'll be a month at least before you do patient-assessment. In the meantime, you can observe procedures, and help with routine tasks. Here is a copy of our work list,' she produced a typewritten sheet. Anne glanced at it quickly, the morning details sprang out: 'Receive report' . . . 'Help serve breakfasts' . . .

'Give out bowls for washing' . . . 'Help with bed-baths' . . . 'Treat pressure areas' . . . 'Quarter-hourly obs' . . .

'Read it later, if you would,' Sister was getting up. 'I'll take you on to the ward now, put you with Staff Nurse Lyne. You'll get to know the patients as you come to do things for them, *and* by reading their medical notes. I encourage all my nurses to do as much reading as they can.'

The inside of Anne's mouth went like dry chamois leather, as she followed Sister's round outline into the ward. It was a terrible feeling passing through those doors; all the beds seemed to merge and stream out into two long lines, one at each side of her, looking watery green because of the curtains, and the floor was a brown ruler, or a brown plank, along which she had to walk. They reached the desk, large and central, which she knew was the nurses' station. It was there that she was introduced to a girl of about her own age. She was wearing the mauve and white dress of a staff nurse; she smiled and shook Anne's hand.

'Welcome to Livingstone, hope you'll like us.'

'I'm sure I shall,' Anne replied. Sister left them together, and Nurse Lyne came round the desk.

'We're expecting an emergency admission,' she said, 'perhaps you'll see to his bed. He's to go in number twelve over there,' she pointed down the ward. 'Make up the bottom in the usual way, the top part into a pack, lay on one pillow, but protect it, he may still be haemorrhaging. Put a bowl and some paper wipes on his locker, and a blood-pressure reading machine. Nurse Tillot will show you where everything's kept.' She called over a second-year nurse, who was helping a patient on with his dressing-gown. 'Show Nurse Pentrose the linen cupboard, Ellen, and the rest of the corridor rooms, but be quick about it, we're running late.' She flipped up her fob watch.

'We're always running late, so that's nothing to worry about,' Ellen Tillot said sotto voce to Anne, as they bustled out of the ward. 'Jane Lyne's not bad to work with, though. She's the junior staff nurse, but watch out for Logan, she's the senior; she's in charge when Sister's off. Rose Logan's the mickey-taking sort.'

'Oh,' said Anne, 'thanks for the tip.' They had reached the corridor, and tramped its length, making for the top. Ellen Tillot was darting and sprite-like, with dark hair and very white teeth, and a look in her eye Anne wasn't quite sure about.

'I'm not trying to scare you,' she added, 'you'll get used to us all in time. Now, how about this guided tour . . .' she began to point out the rooms: 'Linen cupboard here at the top, staff rooms opposite, doctors' interview room next door, clean and dirty utilities, treatment room, bathrooms, ward kitchen, sluice, Sister's office, and the side-wards. You may have noticed a button light over the interview room. That means one of the doctors is in there, most likely Charles Farne. He's gorgeous, distinctive too, got super copper-beech hair. And you know what they say about redhaired men!' She rolled her eyes ceilingwards. 'Our House Physician's a woman—Dr Susan Cleaver. She's just had a baby, so she's still on maternity leave.'

'And I see you two are still in the corridor.' Staff came out of the ward. 'Mr Kent needs help with his catheter, Nurse Tillot. Go and see to him, please. As for you, Nurse,' she looked at Anne, 'if you don't hurry up with that bed, the patient will be trundled into the ward and faced with a set of bare springs! If you need help, ask for it, but don't waste any more time.'

'We've finished, anyway,' said Ellen, forging into the

ward. Staff Nurse Lyne followed her, while Anne retraced her steps to the top of the passage to collect her blankets and sheets.

The size of the linen cupboard amazed her. It was more like a windowless room, the shelves starting at knee level, rising to ceiling height. But everything was in orderly piles, and was easy to recognise. She found all the bedding she needed, and loaded it on to a trolley. Then, steering rather a zigzag course, she got it into the ward. Bed number twelve was just inside the doors. Aware of stares from several directions, she began to make it up. At least this was easy . . . her first real practical task.

The patient in the next bed, a sandyhaired, moonfaced man, looked at her over the top of his *Sunday Mail*. 'Not seen you before, have I, Nurse?'

'I'm new to this ward,' she replied. There was no need to tell him *how* new she was, he would find that out soon enough.

'My name's Malmsbury . . . George Malmsbury.' He laid his paper down flat.

'Hello, Mr Malmsbury,' she smiled at him, but her mind was on her job . . . the drawsheet next, tuck the short end in, pull it tight over the bed, then fold the long end and get it under the mattress without a hump. Good, that seemed to be okay, now for the bedclothes pack . . .

'I'm a diabetic,' Mr Malmsbury went on, 'in here for stabilisation. There are four diabetics in this ward, you know,' he pointed them out to her. 'Tom Pride here, next to me, he's got dry pleurisy—keeps getting hiccoughs, can't talk much, got his side strapped up. Who's going in there, then?' he nodded across at Anne's bed.

'A Mr Anton,' Staff supplied, appearing from nowhere again. She pulled the curtains between the two beds, screening Mr Malmsbury off. 'Yes, Nurse, that's fine,' she said, '*and* just in time as well.' Looking towards the ward doors, Anne saw the end of a stretcher, then its full length as the porters pulled it inside.

Only the face of the patient was visible, a grey and sweating face. The hue of his skin made his hair look chalk white, even his lips were grey. His eyes were closed, but they opened to slits as, with great care and expertise, the porters lifted him on to the waiting bed. A little sharp-featured woman in a bright red knitted hat hovered about until Sister Heyhoe, who had seen the stretcher arrive, entered the ward and took her away to her room.

'We'll soon have you feeling better, Mr Anton,' Staff smiled down at him, as she and Anne unfolded the bedclothes pack. She took his pulse and her face didn't change, but her smile was a little fixed. She asked Anne to raise the foot of the bed. 'And fetch Doctor, if you will.' Her glance at the girl was one of urgency.

Anne reached the interview room in seconds, knocked and went straight in. She burst in. Charles Farne looked electrified. 'Do you usually zoom into rooms like that? If so, why bother with knocking? The whole idea of . . .'

'Dr Farne, Mr Anton has come. Staff said to fetch you . . . can you come quickly? He looks so dreadfully ill!'

'I don't doubt that.' His tone was easy, but he got to his feet at once. His eye passed quickly over the desk. 'Now where on earth did I put . . .'

'If you want your stethoscope it's under that chart.' She reached over and pulled it free.

'Thank you . . . good thinking,' he looped it up, he began to edge round the desk. 'Now all I need, if you'd be so kind, is sufficient room to pass!' His mouth moved in a tight little smile, and she felt her colour come up.

She hadn't realised she was blocking his way, the room was very small; she mumbled, 'Sorry' and flattened against the wall. He squeezed by, but the fit was tight, and she cursed herself for a fool. Why in heaven's name hadn't she gone out first, and left the way clear for him? What a clot she was! She unpeeled herself from the wall. Biting her lips with embarrassment, she watched him walk down to the ward. His head was high, his arms scarcely moved, the stethoscope hung from one hand. Nurse Tillot was right, he was very attractive, but proud and arrogant too, and maybe conceited, with silicon chips for a heart. Still, that needn't be her concern. Anne straightened the bib of her apron, and her cap as well, and hurried back into the ward.

A little uncertain of where to go, she stood near bed number twelve. It was completely enclosed by curtains now, and she saw them billow and bulge, as Dr Farne, accompanied by Sister (Anne could see the back of her shoes) moved within them. The doctor's voice was low. 'Not so much pain now? . . . I'm glad to hear that . . . No, I won't press your abdomen . . . Thirsty, are you? Well, yes, perhaps you could have some ice to suck. No water just for the moment . . . Yes, yes, I know it is . . . Would you like Mrs Anton to come and sit with you, just for a little while?'

'You taken root there or something, Pentrose?' Something hard nudged Anne's ribs, and turning, she saw Nurse Tillot with a tray, on which sat bottles and jars. 'I'm about to do my back rubs,' she said, 'pressure areas. Perhaps you'd like to give me a hand, it's easier with two.'

Anne was just about to agree when Sister's head burst through the curtains. 'Nurse Pentrose, fetch a bowl of ice for Mr Anton, please. Get it from the ward kitchen, and make sure the pieces are small . . . small cubes he can put straight into his mouth.' Her head went back inside again; Ellen Tillot giggled.

'Punch and Judy isn't in it! Well, go and fetch your ice. The second fridge in the kitchen's got a small divided tray, so you won't have to get to work with a chisel!'

For which, thank goodness, Anne muttered, making for the doors, only to be stopped as she passed Sister's office by Staff calling out of it: 'Bring Mrs Anton some tea, Nurse Pentrose, and don't forget the sugar. The lunches will soon be coming down, so you'll have to get a move on.' Anne wasn't surprised to see her look at her watch.

Ice . . . tea . . . back-rubs . . . lunches, and getting to know the diets. Then up to the nurses' dining-room for lunch, meeting other staff. Then back again for the afternoon, Mr Anton on blood transfusion, his bed uncurtained for maximum surveillance; visitors flooding the ward. Grapes being wrested from Mr Malmsbury, whose wife kicked up a fuss. Then going off duty, and feeling punch-drunk, numb with weariness, yet shot through with elation too—a kind of first-day 'high'. And her feet and legs ached—oh, how they ached, right up to her knees. It was because of the parlous state of her legs that when the lift brought her down she decided to short-cut through A and EU (Accident and Emergency). This would, she knew, save the colonnade walk, and would bring her out at the entrance to Cade Street, and Cade House—the Nurses' Home.

The waiting area of the accident unit was more than half full. Patients were grumbling, fretting at having to wait. 'The doctors are all engaged at the moment,' the receptionist was explaining. 'There's been a road accident, there are several urgent cases.'

'So you have to be half dead before you make it through to the cubicles!' a teenage girl shouted out; her companion shut her up. Anne hurried through. She was sorry for them, especially for the children . . . two were crying, and an old man was coughing, making a noise like a rattle; a middle-aged woman was moaning and rocking herself.

Anne fixed her eyes on the exit doors and had very nearly reached them when she felt a kind of jump behind her, and a hand like an iron screw descended on her shoulder and spun her round. At first she thought she'd done something wrong, that someone from the ward— the capricious Ellen Tillot perhaps—had come to sort her out. But the face that was thrusting itself into hers was that of a skinhead youth . . . putty-faced, and reeking of cooking oil. 'Oh no, you don't . . . you 'ent going yet, not yet you 'ent,' he hissed. 'I gotta be seen to, and seen to quick . . . take a look at that!' With his teeth he unwound a filthy bandage from the thumb of his left hand, displaying a cut which opened like a mouth. 'Narsty, 'ent it? Want stitching, don't it? Well, you get on with it, Nurse. I bin waiting a long time, *too* long, and don't look at me like that!' He jerked her away from the wall and back, his right hand tight on her shoulder, his small eyes narrow with menace and pain. As she made to speak, he jerked her again, forward and back in a shake, his fingers biting hard, and her cape lay round her feet.

'I'm sure you'll be seen quite soon now,' she said, trying to keep her voice steady, 'but I don't work on this department, and I'm not allowed to stitch.'

'Oh, don' give me that . . . don' give me that! You're a nurse, you're allowed all right. You see to me now, you see to me quick, or . . .' he jerked her again, sharply and quickly, and she felt her head touch the wall. In no way could it be called a crack, nor even much of a bump, but the feeling of threat, and the egg-shaped head and contorted face inches from hers, was alarming and frightening—yes, even with a roomful of people at very close call. Her heart began to thunder in her ears.

'Let me go, please.' Her voice was steady, it sounded authoritative. The youth's eyes flickered and she pressed her advantage home. 'You'll not help yourself by behaving like this, and you'll probably lose your turn.'

'Shut it, doll! You see to me quick!' The menace was back in his voice; his hand tightened, then a shout made him turn his head.

'Let go of Nurse, and go and sit down . . . either that or leave the department!' From somewhere near—most likely the cubicles—Dr Farne had emerged. He was only a pace or two away, Anne could see him by moving her eyes. 'Out, neck and crop, unless you sit down and await your turn!' he snapped. He had reached them and was standing there ramrod-straight.

The youth swore, his good hand bunched, and Dr Farne slid between him and Anne. 'All right, Nurse, get off home!' She could only see his back; he was facing the boy who, after what seemed like a small eternity, sloped off to the chairs, still hissing obscenities.

'Will they see him? Will they treat him? His thumb is badly cut,' said Anne in gulps, leaning against the wall.

Dr Farne turned round, then almost fell, his feet tangled up in her cape. She bent and retrieved it, ashamed of her shaking hands. 'It's his right to be treated,' he said sternly, 'and it's *your* right to complain. You don't have to put up with that kind of thing. Do you want to complain or not?' The tone of his voice quickly put paid to her shakes.

'No, of course I don't.' She turned to go, 'I was startled at first, that's all. It was something and nothing, but thank you for helping me.'

'You were doing all right on your own, I think . . . handling him pretty well.' He drew her on to one side as

a nurse with a pile of blankets butted herself backwards
through the doors. They passed out into the yard. 'I'll
see you across to the Home,' said Dr Farne, jerking his
chin at the sky.

It was four-thirty in the afternoon and very nearly
dark. The rain had turned to a blowing drizzle, making
haloes round the lamps. The air smelled of London . . .
of diesel fumes, of traffic, and trains, and river. A tug
hooted mournfully somewhere near Blackfriars Bridge.

They began to cross the courtyard, and Anne wished
he would go away; she was beginning to feel a little odd,
and she didn't want him to see it . . . to witness it . . .
after all, she had her pride. He was holding her arm very
tightly indeed through the thickness of her cape. Once
she slipped on some fallen leaves, and he all but held her
up. She knew her cap had come unpinned, she could feel
it slithering back. She put up a hand to stop it, just as
they got to the gates, just as a voice hailed Charles Farne
. . . a voice with a foreign accent; it came from a blue
Cortina at the kerb. 'Oh, there you are, Charles . . . I
thought you were lost, or caught up in some con-tre-
temps!' The last word came out with careful slowness, as
the car window was opened and a girl with fringed yellow
hair looked out. She was attractive, with a wide smile,
that much Anne could see. The diagonal band of her
safety belt lay against pale fur. She sat there looking a
little surprised.

Charles went to the car. Anne had to as well, for he
still had hold of her arm. 'Stay parked right there, Leda,'
he said in his Registrar's voice. 'I'll be minutes only, I'm
seeing Nurse over the road.'

'I will wait,' came the quick reply. The girl rolled the
window up, her pale outline blurred behind the glass.

The road was busy, alive with traffic, it swept along
like a torrent; the noise was deafening. Anne tried to

free her arm. 'Dr Farne . . .' he bent to her, and she shouted into his ear: 'I'm perfectly capable of crossing the road. I'm not in shock, you know.'

'You're resistant to being helped, I know that,' they teetered on the kerb, 'but this time you'll have to suffer it, I intend to see you across.' His jaw jutted, his mouth set, even his nose looked determined. 'We're both of us shouting ourselves hoarse, so let's stop arguing.' And with that he thrust her over the road, weaving in and out of the traffic with calm resolution, and a good deal of panache. It was hair-raising, and yet she felt safe, she had to admit to that. Then up the steps of Cade House they went, into its jam-packed hall . . . alive with nurses. Dr Farne cleaved a way through to the stairs. 'Now see you get some rest,' he said, releasing her arm at last. Anne rubbed it under the cover of her cape.

'Thank you, I will.'

'First days are trying in most occupations, I think.' His sudden smile took her unawares, and she found herself smiling back, feeling in accord with him, and feeling surprised that she did. So, she thought, he can charm as well, he's got everything it takes. As she watched him go to the doors and stab round them, she wondered about the girl. She was most likely his current girl-friend. Women tended to fancy doctors . . . the attractive ones were practically eaten alive!

CHAPTER TWO

'IT seems to me that your day was one long round of drama,' Pru said later when, in the kitchen two doors from their rooms, they were making toast, and scrambling eggs, and getting out pots of yoghourt from the fridge labelled 'Nurses Pentrose and Wayne'. The two girls with whom they shared the kitchen were out for the evening. 'So let's eat in here and save cartage.' Pru served out the food, and they sat down at the table with their plates.

The quickly cooked meal was a great reviver, and Anne thought how lucky she was to have a friend who was such an excellent cook. Scrambled eggs aren't the easiest thing in the world to get just right. If one is not careful they come out all curdy and swimming in beastly liquid. Pru's were perfect—creamy, and golden, and light. 'And as I was saying,' she went on, 'you've had a riveting day. Mine was a round of cleaning dentures and adjusting hearing aids. Nevertheless, in spite of that, I think I shall like geriatrics. Some of the oldies are lovely to talk to—really interesting. And the staff are great. I quite enjoyed myself.

'Good,' said Anne, staring at Pru, who looked cheerful, fresh and bright. She was eighteen, *only* eighteen, so perhaps those extra years—from eighteen to twenty-one—took their toll at the end of the day. Anne's feet and legs still ached unmercifully.

'There's a male nurse on our ward,' said Pru, 'name of Tom Jevons. He's third-year, we lunched together, and he told me about your ward. He used to be on it, he's only been on geriatrics a week.'

'I see.' Anne waited patiently, she could tell there was more to come.

'He says your Sister's getting married next week, to a doctor in Cas.'

'*Is* she? Oh, glory! I expect that means she'll leave.' (And they'd have a new Sister, or an acting one, maybe the one called Logan, the Senior staff nurse, the mickey-taking one).

'She's not leaving,' Pru said importantly, rattling on at speed. 'She's only having a week's honeymoon, then coming back to work. The consultant, Professor Rawston, is giving a party for her at his Hampstead home, on Saturday, I think.'

'She's very likeable.' Anne brought to mind Sister's remarks about her . . . the encouraging ones she had heard outside her room.

'You might get an invite.'

'To the wedding?' Anne's slim eyebrows rose.

'No, silly, to the party. After all, you're part of the ward. According to Tom, Professor Rawston is very decent to juniors. I bet you'll be asked. I can see it happening, I can see it coming off.'

'I don't really think so,' said Anne, 'and I couldn't, at the moment, care less.' Under the table she eased her feet out of her shoes.

But Pru was right, she *was* asked, by Professor Rawston in person, and he gave her no leeway at all to refuse. It came about on the following Thursday, just prior to a ward round, when he and Dr Farne and a clutch of medical students filed through the doors at ten a.m. Staff Nurse Logan hurried to greet them, for she was in charge that morning. Seconds before she had nagged at Anne for being late with her bed-baths: 'Get a move on, girl . . . get tidied up, you'll have to be quicker than this! The doctors are coming, the consultant is on his way up.'

'I've nearly done,' Anne said evenly, wringing out a flannel. She found it impossible, even unkind, to hurry very ill patients. Mr Ronald Stevens, with congestive heart failure, became breathless at the least effort. He could do very little to help himself; he was also, because of his illness, irritable and difficult to please.

Anne ran into the procession of doctors roughly half-way down the ward. It was headed by the Professor, and Rose Logan walked at his side. She glared at Anne and made twitchy signs with her thick black brows. Obeying the signs, which meant . . . Out! . . . *Out!* . . . Anne made to continue her journey, but was stopped by Professor Rawston, who slapped a large hand flat down on her trolley, narrowly missing a slippery piece of soap. 'You're new!' he barked.

'Yes, Professor.'

'Name?' he smiled at her. He was thick and bulky, his jacket buttons strained.

'I'm Anne Pentrose,' she smiled back at him.

'And this is her first ward. She'll be with us twelve weeks, sir,' said Rose Logan smartly, her glasses misting up.

'Splendid!' The Professor's smile showed a row of well-filled teeth. 'In that case you can come to my little gathering on Saturday night . . . six-thirty at my home in Hampstead, to give Sister Heyhoe a send-off. She's getting married on Monday, I'm quite sure you'll have heard.'

'Yes, I have, and thank you for . . .'

He waved an imperious hand. 'No need to thank me, just come along. Now, where were we, Staff? Ah yes, the lung abscess case, swinging temperature, dear me!' Frowning hard, he studied the notes, while Charles

Farne added his comments, Rose Logan looked attentive, and the four medical students broke rank to let Anne and her trolley through.

'Like being descended on by royalty, isn't it?' Ellen Tillot said in the sluice. 'They'll be in there another hour at least.' She switched off the steriliser, just as a step sounded outside, and Nurse Logan's strident voice told her to prepare a trolley for lumbar puncture at once.

'The Professor's taking a specimen of spinal fluid from Mr Potter. Take Nurse Pentrose with you when you lay up the trolley, then send her in with it. I shall want you to watch the procedure, Nurse, then write up your observations. That will be your test for this week. It will go in Sister's file.'

'Yes, Staff.' Anne felt apprehensive and, for once, her feelings showed—not missed by Rose, who smiled and tossed her head.

'You won't have to assist the Professor. *I* shall do that,' she announced, and made off with her usual clumping tread.

'All apparatus must be sterile,' said Ellen, as they went into Clean Utility. She prepared the trolley, but did it so swiftly that Anne found it difficult to recognise all the equipment as it was placed in the metal receivers . . . spirit solution, needles, syringe, a special needle called 'Barker's' with a tap and piece of tubing to fit the side. There was a glass manometer, local anaesthetic, forceps, swabs and dressings, strapping and scissors, labels for the Lab. There were other things too that passed in a blur. 'Off you go,' Ellen urged, 'and for heaven's sake don't overturn it, or run it into the sluice, or sneeze all over it, scattering germs.'

Anne scarcely heard her, she was going down the corridor, heavy trolley chinking. She was nervous, but excited too; it would all be interesting. She had heard about lumbar punctures in Block, she wanted to see one done; she wanted to learn, because that was the whole idea of her being here. She must watch closely and not miss a thing, she must memorise it all. Perhaps she could write her report in her room tonight.

She was puzzled, however, on entering the ward, to find that the Professor, with two of the medical students and the staff nurse, were grouped round Mr Pride's bed. The other two medics were still with Dr Farne, who was talking to Mr Potter. 'Over here!' they called to her, holding the curtains apart, and she went forward, wondering what was afoot.

'The Professor's busy, so I'm dealing with this—put the trolley on the right,' Charles Farne said crisply, seeing her mystified face. He moved to the right of the bed himself, motioning her to the left, while the medical students stood silently at the foot. 'It looks a mite awesome, I know, Mr Potter,' he began to pull on his gloves, 'but there's absolutely nothing to it, and it won't take many minutes. Okay then, Nurse, ready when you are,' he smiled at Anne over the bed. And she didn't believe it . . . couldn't believe it . . . he couldn't mean *her* to help! She stared back at him frozen-faced, and all but shook her head. 'There's absolutely nothing to it,' she heard him say again. She thought he was talking to Mr Potter, but perhaps he meant her this time. And his eyes didn't scoff, nor challenge; they smiled and encouraged her. But even so . . . even so . . . she still felt very unsure.

'Will I feel it, Nurse?' asked Mr Potter, and her hesitation went. She forgot her own fears as she reassured him:

'No, Mr Potter, you won't. You won't feel pain at all, as such, only a little prick, followed by a kind of pressure on your back.'

'Oh well, if you say so, dear.' Mr Potter eased himself up. She removed his pyjama jacket and helped him lie on his side, on his left side facing her, very near to the edge of the bed. Then she drew up his knees and asked him to try to bend his head to meet them. This gave a good round to his back, enabling Dr Farne to inject first the local anaesthetic, then push in the long Barker's needle between the third and fourth vertebrae of his spine. The fluid began to rise up in the graduated jar; it rose more quickly when at Dr Farne's request, one of the medical students gently compressed the big vein in the patient's neck. Anne continued to hold him, and she tried to be reassuring. Touch was everything at times like that; the touch of a hand, or an arm, and the sound of a voice, meant so very much. She was glad . . . thankful . . . to be taking part. She even felt like a nurse. She felt involved in a way she couldn't explain.

'I'm going to take the needle out now. You may feel a very slight pull . . . nothing to be alarmed about, try to keep very still.' Dr Farne sounded very matter-of-fact . . . cheerful as Larry, thought Anne. And then it was over, the needle was out, and a tiny Elastoplast dressing, over cottonwool, was put on the puncture wound. 'Now I'm sure that wasn't too bad, Mr Potter.' Charles Farne handed the specimen over to one of the students, who labelled the jar for taking down to the labs.

'Not so bad, no.' Mr Potter drew breath, raising his head with relief.

Anne laid him flat, removing his pillow. 'Sorry about that,' she said, 'but we want you to lie absolutely flat, just for a few hours. If you get a headache, or feel unwell, press your bell for a nurse.'

'All right . . . at . . . moment . . . slightly stiff.'

'That'll wear off very soon.'

'But what about the result, Doctor?' she heard him enquire of Charles Farne.

'Should get it in a matter of hours, Mr Potter, depending on the labs . . . how busy they are, that sort of thing.'

'But what do *you* think is wrong?'

'That's not a very fair question, you know.' Charles Farne blew out his cheeks. 'I don't like making guesses, but what I *can* promise is you'll have the best treatment we can provide, the best nursing care too. You see, it's a matter of . . .'

Anne left them talking, as she wheeled the trolley away, down the ward, and out through the door, past a surprised-looking Rose Logan, up the corridor to Dirty Utility. There she leaned against the wall and drew several good deep breaths. It was heaven to be on her own for a minute, but a minute was all it was, for Ellen appeared, her sharp little face agog. 'I *say*, I had no idea our Charles was taking that spinal fluid! Did he actually *ask* you to help?'

'He seemed to assume that I would. But I didn't do much, except hold the patient, the medics did most of the helping. Ellen, what do I do with these things? Do Sterile Supply collect them?'

'Yes, of course, but we rinse them first. I'll give you a hand, if you like. Come on now, Annie, loosen up, tell me how you got on. Was he decent to you, nice to you? Did he show off in front of the boys?'

'No, he didn't.' Anne passed the tray of equipment over to Ellen. 'He doesn't seem to be that kind of person, and he was super at explaining. I'm sure he did it for the medics' sake, but I got the benefit too. Now I've got to write it up. Oh, I wish I could do it now . . . right now, while it's still clear in my mind.'

'Well, why don't you? It shouldn't take long.' Ellen's back was turned to Anne—a thin, narrow, feline back, with sticking-out shoulder-blades. 'You used to be a secretary, didn't you, so why don't you type it out? There's a machine in the doctors' interview room—slip in and do it there.'

'Don't be silly!'

'I'm not, I'm serious.' Ellen glanced over her shoulder. 'Who's to know? The Prof and Charles will be ages in the ward, and even when they come out they won't touch the interview room; they'll be off like the clappers to Female Medical. Go on, go and get it done.'

'I don't think so.' Anne's voice was clipped. Ellen's glance at her had been sly. Her suggestion was one which, if taken up, would drop her right in it, she thought. Half of her felt up in arms, the other half wanted to laugh. There was no real harm in Ellen, but in one or two respects she hadn't completely, for all her year's seniority in rank, progressed out of the silly schoolgirl stage. 'The interview room is sacrosanct, Ellen—even I know that,' she said, just as a long shape flicked by the doorway, then flicked back and stayed, looking in. Both girls swivelled round to see Charles Farne. He looked at Anne, who was wiping her trolley down.

'Thank you for your help, Nurse. It was much appreciated.'

'I was glad of the chance to learn,' she said. In the small ensuing silence she heard Ellen slam the lid of the dressing bin.

'I suppose,' Charles cleared his throat, 'you've got a report to do?'

'I'm afraid so, yes.'

'Can you type at all?'

'Yes,' she stared at him.

'Because I happen to have a typewriter . . . a portable, over there,' he indicated the interview room with a backwards jerk of his head. 'You can come in and use it, if you like. I don't suppose you'd be long?' His voice rose in query, he rubbed the point of his chin.

'Oh no, Doctor, I wouldn't be long, and thank you, I'd like to use it.' Her reply came quickly, on the instant; Ellen's face was a study . . . her mouth gaped, as though she were catching flies. 'I'll use my coffee-break time, Ellen,' said Anne, as she walked with Charles Farne across the passage and into the interview room.

He shut the door and opened a window. 'Let me know if you're cold, but this room's the devil to ventilate properly, and our heating's rather fierce.'

'Yes, it is.' She felt selfconscious. Was he going to stay here with her? Surely he'd go and leave her to it, he couldn't be meaning to stay. She sat down at the desk, while he bent to a drawer and pulled out paper and carbon. The typewriter was tugged from a cupboard, and set in front of her, unlocked and divested of its case.

'There you are, then. Fire away!' he smiled at her. 'I've got some telephoning to do, but your clatter won't affect it; my ears are the accommodating sort.'

He was very different from what she had thought. She stole a glance at him as he sat at the telephone table, which let down from the wall. His wrist was uplifted, holding the receiver, his head was a little set back, his profile clear against the pale grey door. The shape of his head was good and strong, so was the dark red hair, which was struggling so hard to curl. His hair was like him . . . vital, wilful, fascinating too. Her thoughts ran amok for several seconds, till she got them assembled again . . . on medical lines; she began to type her report.

She typed for nearly ten minutes, and lost herself in her task. At the end of that time she had covered nearly three foolscap sheets. She thought she had mentioned everything. The report would go to Sister, would be put in the file she kept for each learner nurse.

'Have you any idea of what might show up in that specimen of fluid?' Charles Farne had finished his calls and turned his chair round to the desk; he scanned Anne's report, then pushed it back to her. The professional note was back in his voice, and his gaunt face was deadpan . . . clear and clean of any expression, apart from the merest glint of curiosity as his eyes met hers head on.

'It may show that Mr Potter has one of the demyelinating diseases, or that he's suffering from spondylosis, or has a type of neoplasm.'

'To name but a few.' His fingers beat a tattoo on the desk. His brows knitted, his mouth thinned, then abruptly changing the subject, he asked her where she had learned to type at such a cracking speed. 'You're not a two-finger plonker, are you . . . not like me?' he smiled.

'I trained as a secretary,' she smiled back at him. 'I worked for a publishing house in Melbourne, I liked it very much.'

'Worked your way up, I dare say?'

'Well, yes, you could say that.' She didn't tell him that during the last year of her employment she had run a department with six girls under her. She felt that that particular experience was best kept under wraps. It stood her in no good stead at all, not in the hospital. It is never easy to accept authority when one is used to meting it out, and this was why—only sometimes, of course—she was tempted to rebel, and snap back, when she was ordered about on the ward.

'You must find nursing a drastic change?'

'It's what I wanted to do.' Embarrassed by his perception, she got up and pushed back her chair. 'I'd better go, Doctor. Thank you so much for letting me come in here.' She stretched to pick up her papers, and her hand knocked his on the desk; they both apologised, the contact was fleeting, yet she felt the effect of it so intensely that just for a second her breathing seemed to stop. When she looked up, when she dared to look up, he was jerking the window closed, pulling the arm of the casement, cursing the wreathing fog, which was doing its best to gain entry into the room.

'The season of mists has poetic appeal in the country only, alas. Up here it's nothing but a dangerous nuisance.' He was peering down into the street.

'At least London no longer has smogs.'

'Hasn't had for a long time.' He turned to face her. 'I can't believe you remember those choking smogs.'

'I've read about them, and my father told me . . .' Anne broke off as the door opened and a woman came in—young and pretty and blonde.

'Hello, Charles.' Her voice was light, with a trace of foreign accent. Anne recognised her instantly, even though she was clad in the white coat of a hospital worker, a coat which hung unbuttoned, showing peg-top jeans and a blue and white checked shirt. From one hand dangled a fishmat bag, overflowing with wools and canvases, the other held a picture in a frame.

'Hello there, Leda,' he smiled at her, 'you're wanting Sister, I expect. She's off this morning, and Staff Nurse is busy in the ward. The Prof's still here, finishing his round.'

'In that case I must wait, I suppose.' She set her bag down on the floor. She looked at Anne. 'We have met, have we not? Introduce us, Charles.' Her hair was jaw-length, and ruler-straight, it bounced as she turned her head; she had pale blue eyes, a little too big for her face. Charles moved to stand at her side and performed the introductions.

'Leda, meet Nurse Pentrose, who's on Livingstone for a few weeks. Nurse, meet Miss Eleda Hintzen, our handicraft therapist.'

Leda's handshake was nothing more than a touch, but she stared very hard at Anne. 'When I said we had met,' she went on, 'it was only in passing, of course. It was when Charles was taking you over the road to that awful Nurses' Home.'

'It's a very good Home, as Nurses' Homes go.' Anne felt a shade defensive.

'I would not like it,' Leda declared, turning down her mouth; she looked at Charles putting the typewriter back in its case. 'Do you type as well as nurse?' she asked, her gaze coming back to Anne.

'I do, but typing's not my job, it's only a sideline now.' Anne didn't feel she could stay to explain, for she had just caught sight of the time. If she didn't get back in the ward before Rose Logan came out with the Prof there would be trouble, which she wanted to avoid.

So thanking Charles once again, and edging past Leda Hintzen, she took her report to Sister's office and laid it on the blotter. She peeped in at Mr Potter, as she walked to the ward desk. He was sleeping and looked comfortable, so she left him to his rest, then she helped Ellen Tillot make up her fluid charts. Half an hour later the Professor finished his round and left the ward. Staff Nurse Logan went to coffee, and Ellen took Leda Hintzen to see Mr Malmsbury, who had pegged a mat and wanted to know how to bind it. The up and about patients went to the day room, and not long after that the lunches came down from the kitchens on level five. Anne and Ellen gave them out, carefully checking each one. Three very ill patients had to be fed, and it was after one o'clock before the two girls were free to go to the dining-room for their own meal. By then Sister Heyhoe had come on duty, Rose Logan had signed off, Anne's report was in Sister's hands, and her praise still rang in her ears: 'You've done well, Nurse. This is excellent.' Sister Heyhoe was gratified that her instincts about the Pentrose girl were, so far, proving correct.

Up in the dining-room, over Irish stew and cold apple crumble, Ellen did her best to make amends. 'I wouldn't have let you get caught, Anne . . . in the interview room, I mean. I'd have got you out in good time, you know. I wouldn't like you to think . . .'

'Forget it,' Anne ate her stew, 'I already have. Most new people are the butt of jokes. It doesn't matter a toss.'

'The joke was on me in the end, though,' Ellen remarked with good grace. 'I nearly had kittens when he asked you in, *and* offered the machine!'

'Yes . . . well . . . it was nice of him.'

'He fancies you, I expect.'

'Don't be silly!' protested Anne.

'He probably does . . . he's a sucker for blonde hair. I hope you weren't in a clinch, though, when Miss Zuyder-Zee waltzed in. She's his girl-friend.'

'So I gathered.' Anne chewed on a piece of meat; it was tough and tasteless, and went down her throat like rope.

'She's Dutch.' Ellen passed her the water-jug, and watched her fill her glass. 'They've just come back from a week in Holland, I know that for a fact. There's probably marriage in the offing. They make a good pair, don't you think? Some people say he knew her before she came to the Walbrook, some say he actually helped her land the job.'

'How long has she been here?'

'Six or eight months—he about eighteen. I think he came from Seftonbridge; I'm not sure about her.

They're bound to be at the party on Saturday. You *are* coming, aren't you? The house is at the crossroads end of Fitzjohn's Avenue, so no distance from the Hampstead Underground.'

'You don't have to draw a map for me, Ellen,' Anne pushed her plate on one side. 'I know Hampstead—I used to live there, nearly twelve years ago.'

'You'll find it changed, I can tell you that. You know, Anne, it might be fun. Oh, I don't mean the party, that'll be foul, all speeches and morsels of food. But perhaps we could go on somewhere after, make up our own little group. It's the fifth of November on Saturday; there'll be fireworks, bonfires galore. There's bound to be a display on the Heath, so put your thermals on, and your fire-proof shirt, and prepare for a long, hard night.'

'I'll think about it.' Anne felt her blood chill, and she knew she sounded odd. But Ellen didn't appear to notice, she was hoping for seconds of pudding. She was getting up to join the queue again.

Leda Hintzen was invited to the party, but wasn't able to go. She awoke with a migraine on Saturday morning, and by early afternoon was prostrate in a darkened room in her flatlet in Camden Town. Anne heard Charles explaining this to the Professor when he arrived. 'I tried to ring you earlier, sir, but . . .'

'Been out all day, old man, so's the wife . . . sorry about Leda, hope it's a short attack . . . ergotamine, that's the best thing to shift it.' He gave Charles' shoulder a slap, then wandered away, consulting the notes for his speech.

He delivered it shortly afterwards in the main sitting-room—an oak-panelled rectangular room, with a big log fire blazing in a surround of Portland stone. The guests, who numbered thirty-odd, gathered round in a circle.

There were presents piled on a small table, and after the speech was done, they were handed over to Sister Heyhoe and her fiancé, Dr Grant, by Staff Nurse Lyne, and a Sister from A and EU.

Afterwards the party divided itself into groups. Anne found herself with the medical students who had come to the ward on Thursday. She was also greeted by a solemn young man with a healthy, ruddy face, and a scrub of dark hair as stiff as wire wool. 'I'm Tom Jevons,' he shook her hand, 'and I'm sure you're Anne Pentrose. Pru told me I would know you by your hair.'

Her hair was down, waving loose past her shoulders, swinging when she walked. Her dress was a straight-cut almond green silk, with a gold mesh belt. The mirror told her she looked her best, but that wasn't how she felt. Behind her eyes, calm like pools, behind her smiling face, she was tightly gripped, so much so that she had a job to swallow. The level of wine in her glass remained the same for a very long time. She knew it was a mistake to have come. She should have stayed in tonight . . . at the Nurses' Home, as Pru had wanted her to.

'Why stand when you can sit, Miss Pentrose?' a voice intoned behind her—a deep voice, and one she already knew well. Turning round, she saw Charles Farne looking down at her. He wasn't all that much taller than her, and standing close like this, she could see the way his grey eyes seemed to darken when he smiled, see the lines at his mouth curve into bracket ones. 'Come and sit down.' The palm of his hand neatly cupped her elbow as they walked together to a group of chairs at the side. 'Enjoying yourself?' He crossed his legs and leaned back comfortably.

'Yes, thank you, I am.'

His eyebrows rose, and she knew he didn't believe her. 'You looked as though you weren't all that keen to be ringed by admiring males. Most girls . . .'

'I'm not most girls!' she snapped, and saw his start of surprise. Somehow she had to explain herself, give a reason for being so rude. Even a half-lie, a white lie, would do . . . *anything* would do. 'I'm not used to this formal type of party,' she blurted out in a rush. 'In Australia they're different.'

'Are they indeed? Bigger and better, no doubt!'

Somehow or other she bit back the angry retort that his words provoked. Her face paled with the effort. He leaned forward in his chair.

'I'm sorry,' she heard him say. 'I'm sorry, that was uncalled for.'

'It doesn't matter. It was all my fault.' And now she gulped at her glass, but perhaps the wine had some effect, for the colour returned to her cheeks. He talked about work, which steered a safer course.

'How,' he asked, leaning back again, 'have you liked your first week on the ward?'

'Very much, all things considered, but I still feel very new.'

'A dogsbody too, maybe?'

'That all the time!' she laughed. He looked at her thoughtfully over the rim of his glass of tonic water with its dash of lemon. He never drank and drove.

'A medical ward is a good one to start on,' he continued pleasantly. 'It's the ward where diagnoses are made and treatments are prescribed. There's a good chance to mug up your drugs, and to see a case right through, from start to finish . . . an interest in itself.'

'I agree,' she said, 'and I'm sure I shall like it, especially as I go on. And I'm so glad about Mr Potter. I'm glad he has no disease.'

'Mm, yes, so am I. The result is what I hoped for—something "innocent", something curable, something operable. After surgery and convalescence he'll be going home cured—able to work completely free from pain.'

'Yes.' Anne sat there thinking about it, thinking about Mr Potter. A myelogram (a type of X-ray) done after the lumbar puncture had shown, together with the lab investigation of the fluid, that the patient had a neurofibroma—a benign growth on his spine. This had distended the vertebral canal and caused pressure on the cord, resulting in pain, which had laid Mr Potter low. He had been transferred to Martindale Ward, which was male surgical, and was having an operation on Monday next.

'He's a cricket enthusiast,' Charles went on, 'plays for his county, he tells me. He hopes to do so again next spring, and I see no reason why not. Now, on the verge of winter, the spring seems light years away. It'll come, though, soon enough.' His voice dropped in tone, and glancing at him, Anne thought he looked sad, as though something upsetting had struck him. Not liking to stare, she averted her eyes, then saw to her surprise that the rest of the party were converging on the far end of the room. Mrs Rawston was pulling the curtains' cord and unbolting French doors which appeared to lead out to a first-floor balcony.

'Why are they going out there?' she asked. Charles screwed round to see.

'Next-door's bonfire's the attraction, I think. I believe it's just been lit. I noticed a would-be towering inferno being built as I turned up the drive. We'd better join them, don't you think?' He waited for her to get up. 'It's the fifth of November, in case you've forgotten . . . gunpowder, treason and plot! Now that may be something that your precious Australia fails to commemorate!'

Anne didn't reply, she simply went with him, but she did her best to hang back. Mrs Rawston called him on to one side to help her with a cork. Anne stood by the folds of the curtain, hoping she wouldn't be noticed, hoping she wouldn't have to go and stand on that balcony. But Tom Jevons was looking for her, she heard his raucous shout: 'Hey, Anne, you can't see from there . . . catch hold, I'll pull you through!' She couldn't protest, not without looking silly, so she took his outstretched hand and let him pull her through the crowd to the front of the balcony. She sickened as soon as she saw the fire.

It was massive, newly lit, in the crackling, shooting-up stage. It was sending up billows, towers of smoke, so thick as to look almost solid. The flames were greedy, flickering like lightning, snatching and widening to sheets; they roared and pelted, they gathered heat and strength. She could feel the heat, but the worst was the smoke . . . that searing, acrid smell . . . the smell she had been aware of ever since darkness fell, ever since Ellen and she had emerged from the Tube. It was the smell that brought another scene back, in vivid intensity . . . the scene or sight of a small town half demolished by fire, a town that still smouldered, its timbers white-hot, its buildings blackened teeth, its trees exploding, raining down fire-balls.

But she couldn't . . . mustn't think of that now. She gripped the balcony rail. The bonfire in the garden next door, ringed by excited children, had been purposely lit, was a fun-fire, nothing more.

She tried to turn to go back in the room, but found she was firmly wedged. She couldn't possibly make a fuss, or try to fight her way out. She couldn't move, she had to stay where she was.

The fire was fiercer, hotter, brighter. Anne tried shutting her eyes. She tried looking down at her feet, she tried to transcend the scene. She couldn't transcend it, nothing worked, and she strained to be sensible, but the reek of smoke, the sheets of flame, the pictures it lit in her mind, took her over, battering her like waves.

Even so, she might have managed, might *just* have stuck it out, if one of the medical students hadn't said in ghoulish tones: 'Just imagine how shocking the Australian bush fires must be. They say flames can leap and roar and chase faster than man can run. Imagine running for your life from a holocaust like that!'

Tom said something in reply, but Anne didn't hear. All she heard was her own choking gasp, while the fire-plumed, spark-shot sky began to spin like a Catherine wheel . . . to spin and spin and spin . . . taking her with it, whirling her round, till darkness came in at the sides . . .

And she sank to her knees in blessed oblivion.

CHAPTER THREE

SOUND came back first; Anne heard people talking almost before she was round. 'Did she have too much to drink, do you think . . . on an empty stomach, perhaps?' She wanted to protest at that, then someone did it for her: 'No question of that, I know she didn't.' And that was Charles Farne's voice. Then came Sister's: 'I'm afraid it's more likely she was tired to death, poor girl.' After that Tom Jevons' voice came bracingly into her ear: 'Come on, Anne! Come on, now . . . open your eyes!'

Her eyelids moved, fluttered up. She was back in the room again, being stared at by a sea of faces, or so it seemed just then. Someone raised her head, and a necklace swung close, while a sharp, ammoniac smell assaulted her nostrils, making her gasp and choke: 'Wonderful remedy . . . never known it fail!' the Professor's wife declared, putting her phial of smelling-salts back in her bag.

'Stay where you are for a little while. Please don't try to get up.' Turning her head, which didn't as yet feel it was part of her, Anne saw Charles Farne on her other side, kneeling on the carpet. A glass of water flopped in his hand; some had spilled on to his trousers. She stared at the darkened, spreading patch, as she tried to sip the water. Then she heard him tell the Professor that he would drive her back to the City. 'She can't go by Tube, and I've got my car, and I ought to get back myself. I'm on call, as you know, so when Anne's feeling better . . .'

'I'm better now,' she said. Mrs Rawston helped her

41

into a chair and the Professor brought her brandy. The other guests, at Charles' suggestion, moved away and went on with the party. Some went back to the balcony, but that wasn't her concern, not any more, and she couldn't even be bothered to argue with Charles about his insistence on driving her home.

The fireworks party next door was at its peak as they got into the car. Rockets were tearing into the sky, ending in bursts and bangs and cascades of light, as far out as Muswell Hill. Anne blew her nose and dabbed at her eyes, making Charles glance at her swiftly, as he turned the Mercedes into the Avenue. She was wearing a dark green duffel coat and she had pulled the hood over her head; all he could see was her chin and the tip of her nose. One of her hands moved restlessly up and down the toggle buttons, then clenched in her lap. 'I'm a shocking coward,' she said.

'Nonsense!'

'Oh yes, I am.' She stared out at the lamps, at the king-sized Victorian houses that made up Fitzjohn's Avenue, at the tall trees, still busy shedding leaves.

'In no way are you a coward,' he said in decisive tones.

'You don't know me well enough to judge.'

'I've a nose for that kind of thing.' He drove without speaking till they reached Swiss Cottage, then he took up the conversation as though he'd not left it, as though it were all of one piece. 'You don't come within striking distance of being a coward,' he told her. 'It takes courage to come right across the world to train for a difficult job; it takes sheer guts to emerge with . . . aplomb from a scene with a skinhead youth; it takes courage of a rather more subtle nature to deal with the fears of a patient, right on cue, when you're feeling unsure yourself. We're most of us frightened of something, Anne, but that doesn't make us cowards.'

'The fire made me look back . . . it was more than I could take.'

'Yes, I thought it was that. You once lived in Hampstead, I remember you mentioning it. So did the bonfire make you feel . . . ?'

'Oh, it wasn't nostalgia. I could cope with that, *have* coped with it.' She looked at him, then hesitated; his attention was on the road. She was glad it was, because it made it easier, much easier to talk. He could listen or not, and she could talk and unburden herself. 'I've always had a fear of fire. I was born with it, most likely. It was one of those silly phobia fears, like being afraid of heights, or small enclosed spaces . . . nothing more than that. Now the sight or smell of a fire, especially one outside, takes me back to last spring, when both my parents were killed. They lost their lives in a bush fire in Blandsyde, Victoria. My father was helping the fire-fighters, Mother was out in her car. They were found within yards of each other . . . she must have been trying to reach him. I was in Canberra on holiday, but I got there as soon as I could. I can't begin to describe what I saw . . .' her voice shook, but she carried on: 'Tonight . . . that fire . . . was just enough to bring it all back again. Not that I ever forget it, I try to, but I can't . . . tonight thrust it all back at me, like a flaming torch in my face.'

'Dear heaven! I had no idea!' His comment was nearly inaudible. 'I had no idea . . . none at all!'

'Of course not, I know that,' she said. 'Not many people *do* know, apart from the SNO—Nella, my grandmother, told her when my training was being arranged. She and Miss Rivetts were nurses together . . . years ago, of course. The Director of Nursing knows as well, so does Pru, my friend at the Home. No one else does, I didn't especially want it bandied about . . . not all over the hospital. You know what hospitals are.'

'So *that's* why you left Australia?' His tone was exactly right. She was grateful to him, if he'd sympathised she'd have closed up like a clam, or burst into tears, which might have been very much worse.

'That's why,' she said, 'but I didn't do it without a good deal of thought . . . a great deal of heart-searching too. You see, my home was intact. It happened to be standing in a part of the area the fire didn't reach. As our neighbours said, if only my parents had stayed in the house, they'd have been all right, but of course they didn't. I can just imagine what happened. My father, who had helped before at small, less important fires, would have been off at once to help the fighters, and Mother, as she always did, would have stood the waiting for just so long, and then she'd have got out her car and gone off to find him, because that was the way they were. They had to share, to be together . . . in the end they died together. They'd have wanted that . . . so I hang on to that,' her voice sunk to a whisper, then strengthened again as the dangerous moment passed. 'My grandmother flew out from England. She was with me several weeks. She was Daddy's mother, it was dreadful for her, but she helped me with everything. She's a super person, we've always been close, but we came even closer then. On the night I knew we'd sold the house, we talked together for hours. Nella asked me if I would like to make my home with her in England. She didn't press, or anything like that, just spread the idea out like a set of plans, like blueprints, and we went over them inch by inch. In the end I told her I'd like to come, I couldn't see many snags. Without my parents I had no deep roots . . . there was no one *special* in Australia. I left friends, of course, and I miss them, but we write and keep in touch. Mother's father, Grandpa Lingate, lives in Canberra, so I'm bound to go back one day to visit, when I get proper leave.'

'I expect you made several friends at work?' Charles said quietly. He sounded as though he were trying to assimilate all that she had told him. He sounded appalled, yet as if he were striving not to let it show. His mood was like an extension of her own.

'I made friends at the office . . . yes, of course. I'd known some of them at school.'

'No doubt you were one of those super-efficient, frightening secretary birds!'

'I don't think so.' This made her laugh. 'I just did my job, that's all. When I came back here, while I was waiting for my training term to begin, I was a secretary at Australia House in the Strand, for a time. I commuted from Herts. I was trying to avoid having too much time on my hands.'

'I'm sure,' he managed to say at last, 'that I would have felt the same.'

After that he said very little, she thought because of the traffic, which got heavier as they neared the central zone. He did, however, tell her that his parents lived in Seftonbridge, that he had an accountant brother, Mark, two years his junior, who was currently working out in Johannesburg. It wasn't until they were nearly home, and skirting Smithfield Square, that he asked her how she managed for meals. 'Do you eat at the hospital?'

'Only at lunchtimes, so far,' she replied, 'because Pru cooks at night. I'm hopeless at it, but just at the moment she finds it a novelty. She's doing a paella tonight, so she'll be glad I'm home early.'

'I expect she will,' he said thoughtfully. He drove to the Nurses' Home, where he parked at the kerb, got out and saw her in. 'You're a plucky young woman, Anne Pentrose,' he said as he stood with her at the foot of the stairs—deserted at such a betwixt and between kind of hour.

'Let's just say I'm working on it,' Anne laughed, and her hood tipped back. Her hair clung close to her head and neck, meeting under her chin, scattering in blown tendrils over her brows. She thought he started to say something, then she felt him cup her face, she felt the brief caress of his fingers seconds before he leaned forward and, almost gently, laid his mouth on hers.

Astonishment streaked, streamed into comfort, a strong enveloping tide, a warm rush of masculine solace, sweeping her to an awareness of other feelings far more clamorous. His arms slipped round her, the kiss deepened, her hands moved from his shoulders up round his neck and she felt the thick, crisp hair. Then a door slammed on the landing above, a young nurse called to another, it broke the moment, and Charles let her go, drawing slowly back from her. 'I'd better go before I'm thrown out, I think!' But no smile accompanied his words, and Anne had the feeling, as she mounted the stairs, that he bitterly regretted every shade and nuance of their embrace.

He had kissed her on impulse, she was sure of that—he hadn't intended to do so. He was very likely, right at this moment, as he ran the car into the garage, cursing himself for having let down his guard. On the other hand . . . she reached the landing, forcing her legs to walk . . . he might not be thinking any more about it, he might have flicked it off; he might be hurrying into Residents (he lived at the hospital) to telephone Leda Hintzen to ask how she was. I must dismiss it from my mind, she thought, as Pru called out from the kitchen. I must remember that Nature abhors a vacuum, which is what I'm in at the moment. To be seriously attracted to

Dr Farne would be the uttermost folly. It would be absolutely *asking* to be hurt.

Anne's second Sunday on the ward passed fairly quietly, and without Charles, who very rarely, except in an emergency, came across to the wards unless he was called. On Monday Rose Logan became Acting Sister, and at twelve midday precisely, Sister Heyhoe became Sister Grant, and Nurse Lyne, who had gone to the wedding, came back with a slice of white-iced cake. 'You'll have a job splitting that into six,' said Ellen, eyeing it greedily. But they all had a piece the size of a stamp, and wished the couple luck.

'She's old to be getting married for the first time, isn't she?' Tessa Merrow, the auxiliary, remarked. 'I wonder she's bothering.'

'Who's taking my name in vain?' came in laughing tones from the doorway, and Leda walked in, complete with fishmat bag. She smiled across the ward kitchen, her blue eyes dwelling on Anne. 'Hello, Nurse, are you better? Charles told me what occurred. What a very unfortunate thing to happen at a party. I am so glad he was able to drive you home.'

'Yes, it was kind. I'm fine now, of course. It was nothing very much.' Anne's voice was steady, but the palms of her hands were damp. 'I hope you're better yourself,' she added, 'migraines are fearsome things.'

'Only clever people get them,' smirked Tessa Merrow. Ellen hissed, 'Crawler!' into her ear. Leda looked at Staff Nurse Lyne.

'May I please go into the ward? I've a date with Mr Farmer. He wants to make a string bag for his wife.'

'I think it's all right,' Jane Lyne swept the cake crumbs off the table, 'but just to make absolutely sure, have a word with Rose Logan first.'

'Oh yes, of course, the eth-i-cal nurse.' Once again the foreign inflection was plain to hear in Leda's clear, strong voice. She picked up her bag and went into the passage, and Jane Lyne went with her; the other three nurses, Anne included, watched Leda's buttercup head disappear round the jamb of Sister's door.

Ellen pulled a face at Anne. 'I can never decide,' she said, 'whether I really like her or not. I know she smiles a lot, and she appears friendly, but I get the feeling she looks down on us nurses. When she marries our gallant Registrar she'll be worse than ever, I expect . . . that is if she keeps on working; she may decide to give up.'

'Well, that's their business, isn't it?' Anne said snappily. She refused to be drawn into talk about Charles Farne. Ever since Saturday she had done her best to put him out of her mind. The thought of him marrying Leda Hintzen simply didn't matter, not in the least . . . it was nothing to do with her. He disturbed her, though, and she knew he did; she felt jumpy most of the time. She found herself looking and listening for him, wondering when he would come, or *if* he would come, and how he would be when he did. As she walked along to Sister's office (Rose Logan wanted to see her) her eye was caught by the wall bench, where she had sat last Sunday week and heard him talking to Sister Heyhoe— taking my name in vain, she mimicked, picking up Leda's expression, and hating the sound of it. He had also, it seemed, told Leda all about Saturday. The thought of that stung, because he must have actually *discussed* her with Leda. She bit her lip as she tapped on the office door.

She had only been on duty three hours, she was on the shift called 'lates', which meant that she worked from one p.m. until eight. Rose wanted to brief her on the morning's activities; she also wanted to give her a verbal test.

'I'd like you to tell me as much as you can about Mr Stevens' condition,' she said, leaning back in her chair, looking Anne up and down.

'He's suffering from congestive heart failure, Staff.'

'Yes, and what does that mean?'

'That his heart doesn't empty and fill properly, it doesn't pump as it should. Most of his organs have become congested, including his lungs, which makes him breathless, and his legs have swollen up.'

'His legs and feet are oedematous,' Rose said crushingly, 'his condition is very slow to improve, and to give temporary relief, Dr Farne may decide to draw off some blood, to lessen the strain on his heart. Do you know what that procedure is called?'

'Venesection, Staff. It's like a blood donor giving blood, it's taken out of the arm.'

'Yes . . . fine.' Rose bent her head and scribbled on Anne's report, which was sent in each week to the Nursing School. 'All right, then, Nurse, that's all for now. You'd better go and start teas. Try to get them out of the ward before Dr Farne appears. He's due here in roughly half an hour.'

'Yes, Staff.'

'Well, off you go . . . you're not glued to the floor, I hope!'

'No, sorry . . . I wasn't thinking.'

Rose made a click with her tongue, and Anne sped to the kitchen and took down the big metal urn.

There was no visiting on Mondays, and the ward seemed extra quiet, and extra tidy with no outdoor people sitting round the beds, festooning them with plastic bags and dropping wet on to the floor. It was always raining, or so it seemed to Anne. The only outsider this afternoon was Mrs Floss, the librarian. Leaning forward at a dangerous angle, putting her head down low, she was wheeling her bookcase trolley between the beds. It was a cumbersome trolley, and she puffed and strained, conscious of her gap—the parting of her skirt and jumper, especially at the back. She kept stopping to jerk and pull at the latter, and mop at her hot face, and recommend certain books to the less ill. 'Takes you away on a magic carpet, a good book does. I got through four in a week when I had my gall-bladder out. Now, how about you, Mr Pride . . . you look like a nice thriller.' Hiding a smile, because no one looked less of a thriller than Tom Pride, Anne made slow progression up the ward.

Leda Hintzen was with Mr Farmer, the recovering lung abscess case. She was assembling the hoop for the start of his bag, to be made in scarlet string. It seemed the thing to offer her tea, but she said she only drank coffee. Not feeling she ought to break off to make coffee especially, Anne worked her way to Mr Stevens' bed.

'Thought you was never coming!' he breathed. 'Take your time, you girls . . . chasing your tails, never get anywhere.' He stared at her from his pillows, which propped him up high and helped his chest to expand.

'Now you know that's not true, Mr Stevens.' Anne took her time with him, helping him drink with the aid of a spouted cup.

'You'll soon be jogging round the courtyard, Ron,' George Malmsbury said at her elbow. He had got out of bed to help her with teas, he was being discharged on Wednesday. He had only two more days in Colditz (his name for the hospital) and then he'd be back with his family, able to manage his insulin and his carefully balanced diabetic diet himself. 'Be nice to sleep in my own bed, put my feet on the wife . . . better'n any hot bottle, she is, my Elsie's one of the best. You ought to get married, you know, Nurse, smashing girl like you. Take care you don't end up like Staff Nurse, cold as the virgin snows.'

'Staff can be very kind, Mr Malmsbury.' Anne glanced down the ward at Rose, who was with Mr Anton, helping him into a chair. John Anton was still very weak and ill, but off all parenteral feeding. He was cheerful and grateful for all that was done for him.

'It's something to be able to move about, without being joined up to bottles,' he said, as Anne took him a glass of milk

The phone rang in the office and Rose went to answer it. Minutes later she was back again, beckoning to Anne. 'I want you to get number one side ward ready for a new admission. Nurse Merrow can finish off in here. Come with me, I'll explain.' Anne followed her into the first of the side wards, where she flung open the windows, moving the narrow bed away from the wall. 'He's a young Australian, coming in by ambulance from Dowford in Hertfordshire. Yes, I thought that would make you sit up!' She noted Anne's start of surprise. 'His GP has had him admitted with what he thinks is virus pneumonia. This is the type of respiratory infection which mostly attacks young adults. Make up the bed in the usual way, a pack on top, of course. Get a bed-rest, five pillows, and a Meredith cannula. No, on second thoughts, a ventimask, that would be best, I think.' Her glance went to the oxygen point on the wall at the head of the bed. 'I'm sure you know all the small items for the top of his locker, Nurse. He should he here in twenty minutes, his doctor's letter will be with him, but these details, which I jotted down when Admissions rang through just now, can be put in a folder, to start off his medical notes.' She handed over a slip of paper, which Anne glanced at quickly as she went to the linen cupboard for blankets and sheets.

Hands and thoughts moved in unison, as she made up the bed, as she shut the windows, and made sure that the radiators were working. Ellen came in to check the room, just as the sound of the stretcher-trolley could be heard coming through the corridor doors. Staff Nurse Logan went to meet it; she spoke quietly to the patient. 'Feeling rough, Mr Gilbertson? We'll soon make you comfortable.' By that time the stretcher was in the sideward, and Anne found herself looking at the fever-flushed face of a young man, beard stubble roughening his jaw, hands restless, pushing the blankets back. The transition from stretcher to bed made him gasp, and Ellen reached for the oxygen, placing the ventimask over his nose and mouth. Presently his breathing eased, and the mask was replaced on its hook. 'You'll only need oxygen occasionally in short blasts,' Staff Nurse told him. 'There's nothing to be alarmed about, it's simply to help you breathe.'

He smiled—it was more of a grin than a smile . . . for all the world, thought Anne, as though he found Staff's remark amusing. She wondered why he did. He was young, not so much older than herself, and she felt very protective towards him. Would he get well, properly well, and how long would it take? When she voiced these questions in Sister's office a few minutes later, Rose shrugged noncommittally.

'Viral pneumonia is rarely fatal, if that's what you're asking, Nurse, but that doesn't mean complications can't set in, of course, bronchiectasis being one of them. He'll need very careful nursing. Go and sit with him until Dr Farne comes, and make up a Kardex for him. Apart from his GP's letter (she passed this over to Anne) we haven't much to go on yet, but we can't fuss him with questions. I'll get Dr Farne bleeped, I can't think what's keeping him.' She lifted the telephone, and Anne went back to sit with the patient, Ray Gilbertson.

His eyes were closed and he appeared to be dozing. She pulled up a stool and sat down. His doctor's letter was interesting, she filed it and read it through:

're *Mr. Raymond Peter Gilbertson, aged 28 years*.

Thank you for admitting this patient, whom I consider to be suffering from primary atypical pneumonia. There has been a gradual onset of malaise, headache, muscular pains and cough, temperature rising to 103 deg. There is an area of consolidation in one lung (right). I would add that he is from Perth, Australia, occupation vet. He plans to be here in a working capacity for the next three years. He tells me his health is normally robust, which leads me to the conclusion that his resistance to viral infection has been affected by change of climate. He has been in England four weeks, and is residing with his employer—Mr Harold Lowe, veterinary surgeon, of Dowford, Herts.'

Well, thought Anna, how about that . . . what an amazing thing! Dowford was only three miles from Windon, where Nella, her grandmother, lived. She still hadn't, not as yet, got used to calling it 'home'. Home was still a long, low house, set on a ridge amongst pine trees, in a small town called Blandsyde, Victoria. Anne had never been to Perth, but she had heard it had everything. It was this man's home; she looked across at him. He was looking at her, trying to speak, but instead he began to cough. She waited until the paroxysm was done, standing close to his bed. She wondered about oxygen, but when she reached to the point, he shook his head. 'Okay . . . all right,' he gasped.

'Don't try to speak more than you have to,' she smiled, and touched his hand. 'Dr Farne will be here in a minute. He's clever, and kind, and nice. Respiratory illnesses are something he really gets to grips with. He'll have you well in no time, get you on the right drugs.'

'Hope so . . . damn nuisance.' He started to cough again, just as the door opened wide to admit Nurse Logan. Charles Farne was directly behind her—white-coated and stethoscoped, looking every inch the doctor, looking at Anne on her stool, looking mostly, and lastly, at the patient, Ray Gilbertson.

'All right, Nurse, leave us now,' Rose said quickly. She thrust the stool on to one side the second Anne straightened up off it. Anne made to move behind Charles, but he stood back to give her more room . . . and a keen, quick glance as well, which went through her like a sword. Will I ever, she wondered, ever again, be able to look at him, or even catch sight of him in the distance, even when he's with Leda, without remembering the way I felt coming home with him in the car . . . and afterwards, when he took me in his arms. I never will, never, not if I live to be a hundred. She went next door to the office with fast-beating heart.

The sight of Leda in the easy chair normally reserved for patients, or their relatives, gave her a terrible jolt. 'It's all right for me to be in here, I hope,' Leda leaned back her head and sighed. 'It's exhausting work, teaching, Anne . . . I may call you Anne?'

'Yes, of course you may . . . I mean, why not?' Anne bent to the desk drawers. And I must look the picture of guilt, she thought, and for heaven's sake, *why*? Nothing happened between Charles and me . . . nothing that mattered to *him* . . . which is all that matters to her, surely. And I shouldn't be surprised if she, at times, has fooled around, just for the hell of it. She doesn't look the faithful kind . . . and now I'm being a cat. I wish I'd never set eyes on Dr Farne.

'To learn a simple stitch seems beyond most men,' yawned Leda. 'You'd never believe it, but the geri patients are the quickest to catch on. I've an eighty-year-old in Male Geriatrics who's knitted himself some socks—on two pins, admittedly, but socks for all that.' She was making conversation, being friendly, and Anne did her best to respond.

'I expect you go all over the hospital in the course of your work?'

'To the long-staying wards, yes, I do. I even go to Paeds (children's ward), kids love to crayon and paint. I love children.' She said this simply without affectation. 'So does Charles . . . *fortunately*!' She smiled up at Anne. The smile and the gaze were a little prolonged, then she looked down at her feet. 'I've got to hang on for Acting Sister, I shall probably fall asleep. You couldn't make me a coffee, could you, or is that asking too much? I know how busy you juniors are.' Her toe traced a square on the carpet, and Anne stared at the pink parting crown of her head.

'I'm not rushed at the moment,' she said, 'I'll make it for you with pleasure.' She moved to the door and crossed the passage in two swift strides. I can be just as devious as you, she gritted, and as mealy-mouthed into the bargain. What was she doing, warning me off, or was she gloating, perhaps . . . thrusting her golden future under my nose?

She unscrewed the jar of coffee, plugged the kettle in, took a bottle of milk from the fridge, and closed the door with a bang. They can have a dozen children together for all I care!

I just want to nurse . . . I just want to get people well . . .

CHAPTER FOUR

'THE first year is the worst,' Nella Pentrose remarked, two weeks later, when Anne was at Litchfield Cottage on three days off. 'If a student nurse weathers her first year, she usually carries on. Many give up. Think you'll stick it?' She was mixing the dogs' feed. She bred King Charles spaniels, she had four bitches and a dog—*two* dogs, including Jolly, who really belonged to Anne. He had come from Australia crated up in the plane.

Jolly had only been two and a half months out of quarantine kennels. He still relished and cherished his freedom, he hoped he'd not lose it again. He was six, and Nella had bred him. She had given him to Anne as a tiny pup on her fifteenth birthday, when she had visited England with her father—with John Pentrose, Nella's much loved son.

'There's no doubt in my mind,' Anne told her, 'that I want to keep on nursing. There's something very special about it. It has its own kind of aura. It's just that . . . well, I get homesick sometimes—Australia-sick, I mean.' She threw her grandmother an apologetic glance.

'Well, you've not done anything irrevocable.' Nella tipped mixer meal into the pan of liver and beef and stirred it vigorously. 'By that I mean, if you want to go back, at some time in the future, there's no law to stop you . . . just numerous forms to fill in. All I want is your ultimate happiness.'

Nella Pentrose was a gruff and tough little widow of nearly seventy. She looked her years too, in her baggy old trousers and long hessian apron that she always wore when attending to the dogs. Anne looked at her with affection as she followed her through to the annexe. 'I expect I'll settle down,' she said, 'it's only now and then that I get this stupid wish to back-pedal, usually when something goes wrong.'

'That's when we all question our judgments,' said Nella with a sigh, watching Anne as she bent to fondle the dogs.

The annexe consisted of one large room, floored in quarry tiles. It was kept and used as the dogs' quarters. Nella called it the Kennexe. It was heated along with the rest of the house, and it led out into an orchard, where the dogs could chase each other round the trees. They were also taken on a daily lead walk, all six of them, by Nella, through the country lanes and woods of Hertfordshire. Jolly lived as a pet in the house, he had that privilege. He had recently been mated with one of the Kennexe ladies, and expected to see the results around Christmastime. 'I'd love to be here when the pups are born.' Anne stroked Jolly's mate. Her name was Queenie, she was like him to look at, but milder of expression. Jolly's dark eyes had a knowing, wicked gleam.

'You'll be on duty at Christmas, I expect, but maybe off for New Year, if things are remotely like my day.' Nella picked up the empty bowls. Anne let the dogs out into the orchard, where Jolly very soon joined them. Their excited barking cut through the shivery air. It was exceptionally cold for mid-November, the bleak damp weather having hardened up to bitter overnight frosts. 'We might even have a traditional Christmas. How long is it since you've seen snow?' asked Nella, her eyes on the steely sky.

'Eleven years, probably twelve.' Her grandmother,

asking that, reminded Anne of a conversation she had had with Ray Gilbertson, who had never, he said, seen snow in the whole of his life. Ray was making a good recovery from his viral pneumonia attack. Under Charles Farne's unremitting care the lobe of his lung had cleared and he was off all antibiotics; he might be discharged any day. He wanted Anne to meet him, out of the hospital, once he was discharged. 'Wait until you *are* discharged, and then see how you feel,' she had told him smilingly, but ever mindful of patient/nurse rules and of Staff Nurse Logan, who was just outside the door.

'It's nearly one o'clock!' exclaimed Nella, breaking into Anne's thoughts. Her piercing whistle brought the dogs pelting in, after which she and Anne went through to the house to have their lunch.

Litchfield Cottage was seventeenth-century, apart from the newish annexe. It was built of stone, and was said to have its own ghost. When Nella and her husband had bought it, twenty years ago, the vendors had told them that the ghost of a little old lady haunted the house, and was said to appear in times of great happiness. The vendors had never seen the ghost, but had heard the harpsichord music that was said to surround her, the night their daughter was born. 'But I,' Nella ruefully told anyone who enquired, 'have never seen her, nor heard her music, or at least I haven't *yet*.' She still lived in hopes of doing so, she wasn't the type to scoff. She was fully prepared to believe there were happenings that had no rhyme or reason—happenings that couldn't *always* be explained.

Anne told her grandmother about Ray a little later on, while they ate their lunch in front of the sitting-room fire. 'I don't go to Mr Lowe's surgery,' said Nella, crunching celery. 'Will Grainger's my vet, as you know, but I've met Mr Lowe socially. His practice is very large and widespread, I expect he's glad of some help.'

'Apparently he and Ray's father were friends, years ago,' Anne told her. 'They went to veterinary college together. Mr and Mrs Gilbertson emigrated a year before Ray was born.'

'He's Australian born and bred, then?'

'Yes. He's not been to England before. He's here to widen his experience of small animal care. When he goes back to Perth in three years' time he'll have a partnership . . . within his father's firm, I think he said.'

'I take it he's unmarried?' Nella raised a greying brow.

'Divorced.'

'Pity . . . young for it too.'

'There's no special age for it, darling. Ray lives with the Lowes, he has rooms in their house, he meals with the family, of course, but although he's not lonely, I think he feels odd man out. He's not met many people here yet.'

'Well, that will be taken care of in the fullness of time, I should think. If he's as personable as you say he is, and he gets back his health and strength, he'll integrate into the social life of Dowford soon enough. It's a town that's becoming quite razzmatazz, I'm thankful I live out here.' Nella looked with considerable satisfaction at the vista beyond her windows. They began to talk of village happenings, and the subject of Ray was dropped. Anne didn't mind, but she had the feeling that Nella had swerved the talk with a certain amount of firm deliberateness.

'What sort of a weekend did you have?' asked Ellen, when back on the ward on Monday, Anne and she were busy making beds.

'Thoroughly lazy, I was spoiled rotten, I enjoyed every minute of it.'

'No fewer than two males asked after you. What it is to be missed!'

'Two patients, you mean?' Anne lifted the cradle from Mr Stevens' legs.

'One was a patient—your friend from down under,' Ellen meant Ray Gilbertson, 'while the other,' she added quickly with one of her sly glances, 'was none other than our eminent Registrar.'

'Really?'

'Yes, really,' she mimicked; Anne's calm face didn't deceive her. 'He fancies you, I can tell he does—I expect he's got you in mind for a last mad fling before he sinks down into marriage.'

'I see.' Anne mitred a corner, keeping her head down low. 'Well, it's just as well to know what's in store for me, I suppose.' She hoped Ellen would shut up, for apart from *what* she was saying, she didn't like talking over patients, as though they were lumps of dough. It didn't take much of an effort to include them in surface chat. And Mr Stevens was chipper this morning, not nearly so breathless as usual.

'Dr Farne took some blood from his arm on Saturday,' Ellen explained, 'that's made his congested feeling less . . . at least for the time being.'

'I know it might not last, Nurse,' Mr Stevens put in, 'but I told the doctor . . . I told him, I did, anything's better than nothing . . . anything's better than nothing, sir. Try anything, I said.' He showed the two girls, with considerable pride, the strip of Elastoplast on his inner arm. 'Wonderful what they can do!'

'I bet you're glad he's stopped using leeches!' Ellen said with a grin.

Anne felt revolted, but tried not to show it, because Ellen was showing off. She often did, and in such a mood she was apt to be very trying. She wasn't sorry when Staff

Nurse Lyne called across the ward:

'Can one of you come and help me with this?' She was dismantling an oxygen tent, taking it off a now almost well broncho-pneumonia patient.

'You go, I'll carry on here,' Ellen said bossily, and Anne went, glad of the chance to escape.

A few minutes later, on her own in the sluice, she disinfected the tent, washed it, and began to wipe it dry. She was still trying to sort the flaps when she saw Ray Gilbertson open his door and start to cross the corridor to the bathrooms. He was wearing only pyjama trousers, and she told him off about it. 'The hospital may be warm, Ray, but you've just had pneumonia!'

'Do you think I don't know it!' he said good-humouredly, looking in at her. His triangular face with its jutting cheekbones, his slope of sun-bleached hair, not to mention his ear-to-ear grin, was a cheering, wholesome sight. 'I've missed you,' he said, 'three whole boring days of no see.'

'Get your dressing-gown. Why take risks?'

'Anything you say.' But he didn't *do* as she said, she noticed. He continued his way to the bathrooms, striped towel slung about his neck.

Oh well, so be it, she thought. I doubt if he'll take any harm. He wasn't going to be ordered about, now that he was well, or almost well, and who could blame him for that? She knew she would miss him when he had gone. He aroused all her caring instincts. Not that he'd been a model patient, very far from it; he was impatient, and anxious to get back to work.

The clock on the chapel, inside the main gates, began to strike the hour. Heavens above—ten o'clock! The ward round would start any minute. Charles would be coming . . . *Dr* Farne would be coming, she made the quick correction. She wouldn't be needed, she never was, but all the same, she thought, I'd rather be ready, just in case. There might be something he wants, even if it's only to nod in passing. She'd not seen him since last Thursday. There *could* be something he wanted to say to her.

She began to lift the oxygen tent back on to its frame. It would dry all the better like that, but limp, and damp, and warm, it clung about her, sticking to her arms. Oh, blow the thing . . . she pulled it free.

'Want any help with that?' It was Ray Gilbertson, back again, washed, shaved, brushed, still half naked, and he shouldn't be in the sluice.

'I can manage, Ray—and you're out of bounds!' she scolded.

'You make it sound like a school!'

'It's not unlike, in some respects. Please go back to your room. You'll get me in terrible trouble if not. The doctors' round's due to start, and if Sister catches you in here . . .'

'I'll be spanked, like a naughty boy! Okay, not let it be said I cause trouble, especially for Nurse Pentrose.' He turned to go out, and Anne never knew exactly what happened then; he appeared to trip, to lurch, to flounder, to fight to keep on his feet. She had a split-second's view of his flailing limbs and unbalanced body before he pitched forward and hit the floor with a sickening, bumping thud and a cry of pain that brought her to his side.

'Don't move . . . just stay there! Don't move . . . I'll get Sister! No, Ray—no, don't move!' He paid no heed, but rolled to his feet, stood upright clutching his arm, his right arm, which looked very strange indeed. He was grunting, choking, gasping with pain; he stiffened as Anne touched him, as she put her arm round him and guided him to a chair. She could see what was wrong, she could see what had happened, she recognised the injury; she had seen it before, and dealt with it—on a cricket field in Queensland. He had dislocated his shoulder, wrenched his arm out of its socket . . . it hung forward and his head leaned to the side.

She bent to him, speaking, making him listen. 'Your arm's not broken, Ray, it's dislocated, I can right it, but you'll have to co-operate. It'll take several minutes, but once it's back the pain will go at once.'

'Get on with it . . . *do* it!' His eyes were closed, tears squeezed out of the corners, sweat trickled down from temples to jaw, his skin was greenish-white.

'Put the bottom of your spine right back against the back of the chair, nice and upright—that's fine, that's great. Try to keep perfectly still.'

She lifted the arm to the level of the shoulder, feeling its heavy weight. Her left hand grasped his wrist, turning it up and outwards. Her right hand grasped the point of his elbow . . . now for it, she thought. Please, please let me do it right . . . please don't let him move. Keeping the wrist held up and outwards, she began to pull the elbow—the point of the elbow, sideways across his chest. Slowly, slowly . . . take care, don't rush . . . pull, pull, pull. Oh, come on, get there . . . get there . . . get there! And then she heard a crunch, the sound of the movement of bone upon bone, of the head of the humerus nudging against the rim of the socket. Now to get it in . . . now to get it to drop and slip in. She stopped pulling the elbow; instead she turned her attention to her left hand which still grasped his wrist. 'Nearly there, Ray, hold very still!' She moved his wrist over and inwards, to point towards his left shoulder . . . and then she felt it give, she heard another rubbing grate, and then it was all over . . . it was over and done, the arm slotted back into place.

'God Almighty!'

'I know . . . I know!' She wiped Ray's streaming face. He moved his arm gingerly, tried to grin. 'Does it hurt?' she asked. 'Have you any pain?'

'None, it's gone! Completely all right!' But reaction was setting in. Shocked, trembling, gratitude-filled, he put his arms round her waist and rested his head on the front of her apron. 'You're a miracle-worker,' he told her.

'Nothing like, I regret to say.' Anne felt very shaky herself. 'You must get back to bed, and I must tell Sister. You'll need an X-ray, I expect.' It was then, as she turned with her arm about him, that she saw Sister Grant and Charles Farne advancing into the room.

'What's happened, Nurse? Did you faint, Ray?' Sister's round face looked dismayed.

Charles Farne was more abrasive. 'What the devil's been going on?' He looked at Ray's strained face, at the tipped-over oxygen tent, at Anne with her cap slipping off, her arm round Ray Gilbertson's waist. 'Did he fall? What happened?'

Anne explained, as briefly as she could. She explained what had happened, and what she had done, but she faltered towards the end. The look on Sister's and Dr Farne's faces had changed from merely surprised, to incredulous, to starkly horrified.

'You . . . did . . . *what*!' Charles exploded. She stared at him aghast; she stared at him, holding his eyes, feeling as though she were dropping down, dropping, and tumbling, and rolling into a pit. She'd been rash, impulsive, foolish, crazy. She should never have touched a patient, not like that, so why hadn't she thought . . . why hadn't she stopped to think? She hadn't because, in the face of Ray's pain, all she had thought of was stopping it, and she had known how to. She had once before seen an arm like that, and put it right, as Ray's was all right. She drew threads of courage from that.

'I've done it before, once before in Australia, so I knew how to go about it,' she explained.

And she couldn't, had she known it, have said anything to infuriate him more. As his face darkened, as the world seemed to dwindle to just Charles Farne and her, she heard as if through muffling glass Ray's protesting voice: 'Well, don't blame her, don't knock her, for goodness' sake! I'm perfectly all right. She was great . . . put me out of my misery. I'll never forget what she did!'

'Come back to bed, Mr Gilbertson.' And that was Sister, of course, bundling him out, taking him out. The door of the sluice closed, leaving Anne alone with this man whose anger was like an attack, a thunderous battery of words far worse than blows.

'I don't think,' at first his sentences ground out with dragging slowness, 'that I have ever . . . ever in my life, in the whole of my medical experience . . . heard anything like it, ever once before. You . . . you, a learner nurse, a novice on this ward, have dared to interfere with a patient . . . a patient of *mine*!'

'But that's simply not true!' Her own anger rose, licked into flame by his.

'You interfered! I repeat, *interfered*, risking heaven knows what complications . . . complications and damage, putting a patient through stress!'

'But I knew the injury . . . I'd seen it before!'

'Yes, Nurse, so you said, but this is England . . . London, England, it's not the Australian bush! In case it may have escaped your notice, we have *facilities* here. One floor below where we're standing now is a modern X-ray department. On the same floor we have minor ops and local anaesthesia. Dislocations are reduced there . . . reduced by qualified staff. We don't go in for, neither do we tolerate, little quack osteopaths bent on doing their own thing on the wards!'

'If his arm hadn't been put back fast, the muscles would have gone into spasm. The longer it was left, the greater the spasm.'

'Are you trying to teach me my job?'

'No, Doctor, but you can't expect . . .'

'Now, you listen to me . . . you listen to me, young woman!' He came close, and she saw his arms move. Just for a second she thought he meant to seize her and shake her hard. She didn't even care if he did; she stiffened and stood her ground, and he moved back a little and his hands fell clenched at his sides. 'You listen to me,' his voice throbbed hard. 'If complications arise, if anything untoward arises from what you did just now, Gilbertson could sue, could make a claim against the hospital. Sister would bear the brunt of the blame, because she's in charge of the ward. *You* would most likely get off scot free, but make no mistake about it, *I* would blame you. I would lay the blame firmly at your door.'

'I don't doubt that for one moment.' Anne stared at his thundercloud face, at the furrows of anger, drawing his brows, at his long mouth thinned to a line. If he could, he'd bite my head off, she thought, and laughter rose thick in her throat . . . wild hysterical laughter; she fought to choke it back.

'What was Gilbertson doing in here anyway? Did you invite him in? Were you fooling around, scuffling together? Was that how he fell?'

'It wasn't! And that's unforgivable . . . insulting! Ray Gilbertson's not like that. And neither am I, believe it or not! He came in to help with that.' She pointed to the oxygen canopy on the floor.

'I see,' he said. He looked unconvinced, which seemed the final straw. Anne threw caution, politeness

and deference to the winds; her green eyes flashed, spots
of colour, peony bright, stood out on her cheeks; she
even rose up on her toes as though to try to match his
height.

'I do have *some* sense, Dr Farne, I have enough to
realise that whatever explanation I give, you'll stamp it
out like a light! You won't give it credence . . . you'll
shut your ears, you'll stand and shout me down. So
there's no point in saying more. I'm going back on the
ward. I'm busy, and I haven't . . .'

'I'd like you to wait in my office, Nurse Pentrose.'
Sister's voice cut between them. Unseen and unheard by
either, she had opened the door of the sluice and come
quietly in. 'Go to my room and wait for me, please.' She
dismissed Anne with these words, then her glance went
to Charles. 'I've sent Mr Gilbertson down to X-Ray,
Doctor. I assumed you would want that?'

'Yes—er—thanks,' Anne heard him say, as still
suffused with anger, she crossed the passage and went
into Sister's room.

Once there she stood by the window, aware of her
pounding head and her thudding heart, and of desola-
tion wrapping her like a shawl. She would probably be
given notice. Sister would make a report, the report
would go to the Nursing School, to the Director of
Nursing Education. She'd be given the sack, and that
would be the end of her nursing career—her chosen
career, that had never got off the ground.

Down in the courtyard the fountain was playing,
sending up fronds of water, high and plumed, like
feathery pampas grass. Over towards the main gates,
opposite the Chapel, she could see the uniformed
porters in their lodge. Everything outside was going on
perfectly normally. Inside, and behind her, Sister was
entering the room.

Now for it! Anne stiffened herself for yet another attack. None came. Sister motioned her to a chair. 'Tell me what happened, from start to finish, leave nothing out,' she said. 'I won't ask you to stick to the truth, because you're not a dissembling type, nor a liar. Well, come on—I'm waiting, Nurse.'

So Anne told her story, feeling resigned to whatever might be the outcome. Sister listened intently, she even made notes, and every now and then her violet-blue eyes did a quick summing-up of the tense young nurse in the chair, or *on* the chair; she was right on the edge of it. 'You've been extremely foolish, Anne,' she said at the end, 'foolish, rash and impulsive. You didn't stop to think. Rash behaviour, impulsive actions, have no place in hospital wards. We act with the benefit of knowledge an experience. Mostly we act on orders, we obey rules. We don't rush in where angels fear to tread,' she smiled faintly, then quickly sobered again. 'I shall have to report it to the Nursing School. I'm sorry, but there it is.'

'Is Ray . . . Mr Gilbertson, all right?' asked Anne anxiously.

'His X-ray will tell us that.'

'Will I be given notice?'

'A warning, more likely, I think.' Sister was writing again. Anne stared at her hand, at her left hand on the blotter—a small white, plump hand, wearing a wedding ring, new and gold, symbolic of love, and partnership, and trust. How could Charles Farne have said the things he had?

'All right, Nurse,' Sister finished writing, 'get back to your duties. You're on a split shift today, I see,' her eyes went to the roster.

'Yes, I'm off at twelve, then on again from three till six-thirty.'

'If you take my advice you'll go out at midday . . . get

right off the premises, have your lunch out, give yourself
a break. And don't go doing anything silly, like giving in
your notice. Don't cut off your nose to make a gesture,
because despite what happened just now, I still think
you'll make a fine nurse when you've learned to stick to
the rules.'

'Thank you, but . . .' They both turned round as a tap
on the door heralded the arrival of Ray Gilbertson, his
right arm in a sling, his left hand holding his X-ray films.

'They told me everything's okay,' he said, his glance
going to Anne. 'I've been advised to wear this,' he
pointed to his sling, 'for about a fortnight, and to rest the
arm all I can. Thanks again,' he said to Anne, partly
because he meant it, but partly for Charles Farne's
benefit—he had just come into the room.

'I'll help you back to bed,' Anne made to go out with
Ray.

'Nurse Tillot will do that,' said Sister, 'I want you to go
to the pharmacy.' She handed Anne the prescriptions
Charles had signed.

'You must have flipped your lid,' said Ellen, when
they met later on. 'To reduce a dislocation . . . and you a
learner nurse! You'll get in terrible trouble, you know,
from higher up the scale. Sister Tutor will have your guts
for garters. You'll probably get the push.'

'Shut up, Ellen!' snapped Anne. 'I've just about had
enough!' She was glad beyond measure when twelve
o'clock struck, when she dived into the cloakrooms and
reached up for her overcoat and hat.

She walked almost unseeingly for the first twenty
minutes. Her steps took her to Ludgate Circus and Fleet
Street, and a bar, where she queued for a coffee and
found a vacant stool. To eat was an impossibility, she
didn't even try. She couldn't have got anything solid past
the lump in her throat that filled it like a rock with jagged

teeth. Charles Farne's furious words still made her crumple up. He had lost his temper, she realised that, but even *counting* that, need he have been quite so unfair, so unjust, and so undermining? How could a man who had been so kind (she recalled the night of the party) have a side like that—sarcastic and cruel, and rude . . . yes, *rude*, because that was what he'd been—accusing her of fooling about with Ray. Scuffling, he'd said. How dared he . . . how dared he! He wasn't worth bothering about.

She went to the counter for another coffee, and drank it standing up, watching the snarling tide of traffic passing the *Daily Express* building. It didn't matter what Charles Farne thought, he was nothing to do with her. In another nine weeks, unless she was slung out of the Nursing School, she would be allocated to a different ward, as part of her nursing curriculum. She wouldn't see him nearly so much then, perhaps not at all. She wouldn't have to mind what he thought—what he thought of her. She was only on Livingstone Ward in passing, and perhaps it was just as well that he'd shown this vituperate temper of his fairly early on. Perhaps now she'd stop being so affected by him, so entangled and fascinated. Surely the very last threads of entanglement must have snapped this morning, when he'd turned on her and spat out those awful words. His eyes had gone dark in anger, in temper; the whole of him had blazed; even his hair had seemed to flame, to go more red than brown. But now, of course, she was being fanciful.

She felt better as she left the snack bar, as she cut down Bouverie Street and walked along the Embankment, brisk and hard for half an hour. The exercise, the traffic noise, the slap and smell of the river, the spanning arches of Waterloo Bridge, restored a kind of balance. Even the sight of the red London buses ploughing their way past St Mildred's was a reassurance; they'd been doing it for years.

I'll survive, she thought. I'll get by, I won't be annihilated by the blaming words of a man I don't even like. And as for the row that's brewing, let it rise up and come. But once it's over, I'll put it behind me and start all over again. Even if I'm given notice, I can get another job, in some place, somewhere. I come of fighting stock.

She turned and began to walk back to the hospital.

CHAPTER FIVE

THE summons to Sister Tutor's office came at three-thirty next day. Her comments were short and sharp and to the point. She used phrases like 'walking disaster areas', meaning Anne herself; she expressed shock and profound horror that on her very first ward one of her learners could have acted as she had. 'As it happens,' Sister Tutor's bust heaved, 'no great harm has been done, but even so the fact remains that you acted in a manner quite foreign to the way we like to go on at the Walbrook Hospital. You acted entirely *unprofessionally*.'

There was more on these lines, but no warning was given, there was no question of notice, no threat of dismissal; Anne returned to the ward relieved. The other nurses were all anxious to know how she had got on, including Rose Logan, who had been off duty when Ray had had his fall. To Anne's surprise, she hardly said a single blaming word, just ticked with her tongue and lifted her eyebrows up.

There were ribald comments from one or two patients. 'If I put my knee out, Nurse, will you come and click it back, and rub it afterwards?' . . . 'Can you come and look at my tonsils, love . . . I might want them taken out!'

Ray thought the whole thing was lunatic. 'All this fuss!' he complained. 'If you'd done me any harm, well, then I might have understood it, but you didn't; you did all the right things.'

'They were ethically wrong,' smiled Anne. Ray said

something unrepeatable as she handed him his tea. He was in the day room with several others, conspicuous by his sling, which he took off when the nurses weren't about. He looked young—tall, thin and pale. He needs looking after, she thought, someone to care for him properly. Not for the first time she found herself wondering what his wife had been like, and why they had broken up after only five years of marriage. Anne held the old-fashioned view that marriage should be for ever, and she had not as yet met anyone she would want that commitment with. There had been two people in Melbourne whom she had liked tremendously, but liking wasn't loving . . . there was a whole world of difference. But could one love without liking? Now that just might be tricky . . . risky too. How complicated human relations were! Once again she looked at Ray . . . he needed to put on some weight. He was drinking his tea, and agreeing to play chess with Mr Anton. Leaving them to it, Anne went back into the ward. This was the day for her late shift, so she wouldn't be off until eight, and between then and now she had a whole succession of jobs to be tackled. There was no time for dreaming on the ward.

She was late signing off and the two night nurses were already at the ward desk, as she made her way up the dimly-lit corridor. She was about to pass through the doors to the landing, and thence to the lifts, when she heard a sound in the doctors' interview room. Automatically her eyes went to the wall above the door. No button light was burning—now that was very odd. When one of the doctors was in there, the light was always on. The room was private—sacrosanct, as she had once remarked to Ellen. There had been one or two instances just recently when people from the street had made their way into the hospital buildings, and the staff had all been asked to keep their eyes skinned for intruders, especially at night. Would an intruder come to the fourth floor? Surely that was unlikely. But the fact remained that whoever was in that holy of holies room *shouldn't* be, had no business to be, and with these stoking thoughts, Anne put her hand on the knob and flung the door wide.

The shock when she saw who was seated at the desk was worse than discovering a burglar. It was Charles Farne, in his shirt sleeves, bony face a-scowl, trails of black and red typewriter ribbon heaped on his hands and arms. 'Dr Farne!' she managed at last. 'I thought you were a burglar . . . the button light's not on outside.'

'Bulb's gone!' he growled. He glanced at her quickly, then back at the typewriter. 'I'm trying to fit a new ribbon. I can't get the spool to click into place, and as usual I'm in a hurry. I've got an article on endocarditis to get off to *The Lancet*. I was probably over-ambitious in trying to change the ribbon, but the old one's got holes in it in parts.'

'I noticed that when I did my report on lumbar puncture,' she said, hoping he wouldn't discern the silly nervous shake in her voice. Meeting him so suddenly for the first time since the rumpus, for the first time since he'd blazed at her for 'interfering' with Ray, was disconcerting; she had had no time to prepare.

He raised his head and their eyes met. Anne was still in the open doorway, but even over the three yards distance she could see the black on his face, *and* on his fingers; he held them up with a grimace. 'I'm not good at this sort of thing, alas. I've been fiddling with it for ages, for at least twenty minutes, and I'm damned if I know what's wrong.'

'Changing ribbons is inclined to be messy. Everyone puts it off.' She reached for the knob of the door again and began to pull it towards her. She must shut the door, shut him in, shut herself out in the passage. If she didn't she might be weak enough to actually offer to help. And if she succumbed, how would it look . . . as though she were currying favour, as though she were bent on getting back in his good books. The door had very nearly clicked to when she heard his urgent shout:

'Nurse!'

'Yes?' She pushed the door open, not especially quickly. There was no need, she felt, to start jumping through hoops at the mere sound of his voice. He looked anxious, upset, a little entreating, and she knew the battle was lost. She was weakening already, she could feel herself melting; he had only to ask for her help, and she'd have to give it, she'd have to cave in and say yes. But he'd still got to ask, she wasn't offering, so perhaps the very last dregs of resistance, or common sense, hadn't deserted her.

'Are you in a rush to get off, Anne?' he asked.

'No.'

'Then would you help me with this? You know about typewriters, don't you? I wouldn't ask you, but . . .'

'I'll look at it, certainly . . . only too pleased.' Anne advanced into the room. Charles got up from the chair and held it back for her to sit down. She laid her cape down on the floor and bent forward to the machine. He had a brief view of her neatly coiled hair shining under the light before she turned and looked up into his face. 'You've bought the wrong ribbon, the wrong group number; that means the spool doesn't fit. You won't be able to use it.' She looked back at the machine. Her voice sounded muffled. He left her side and walked round to the front of the desk.

'So does that mean,' he cleared his throat, 'that I'll have to refit the old one?' He swooped down to the waste-paper bin and come up holding the ribbon. He looked red and abashed; he pulled out his hanky and scrubbed away at his fingers. 'Damn filthy job! I know nothing about machines!'

'Well, you can't be good at everything, can you?' Anne held out her hand for the spool. 'I'll rewind the new ribbon on to it. It'll take a little time and a little patience, but I'll get there in the end.'

'It's good of you.'

'Think nothing of it.' She began to take the old ribbon off the spool, spinning it down like a yo-yo, getting as messy as he had.

He sat down at the telephone table when she started the re-winding. She couldn't forget him, not for an instant, and the ticking burr of the spool, as she turned it round, ratcheted in her head. He knows the effect he has, she thought, and he uses it for his own ends. He's physically attractive, remorselessly so; it gets him what he wants, even if it's only a minor thing like fitting a typewriter ribbon. But I'm not typing his article for him—that I will not do. For one thing his handwriting's worse than awful, and for another I want to get home— safely home, completely out of range.

As she bent closer to hook the ribbon through its bracket holder, she risked a quick glance in his direction, and found him looking at her. Immediately, as though he had touched her, she felt emotion flash like little needles slivering under her skin. You've finished, she told herself, tell him so, and go:

'I've finished, and it's all right. You'll have no trouble now.' She got up so swiftly that her chair tipped back on the floor.

'I can't tell you how grateful I am.'

'I'm glad I was able to help.' Anne picked up her chair, and her cape as well, and moved round the end of the desk. Charles was standing in front of the door but didn't attempt to open it. 'I'll say good night, then.' She smiled stiffly, hugging her cape to her chin.

'Am I allowed . . .' his hand touched her shoulder, 'to raise a sore subject, Anne?'

'If it's about yesterday, Doctor, I'd really rather you didn't. You see, I feel . . .'

'You see, *I* feel I can't take back what I said. You were wrong, and I was right, but I shouldn't have lost my temper. I came over too strong . . . I'm apt to do that, it's a very bad failing of mine.'

He had apologised, not fulsomely, but adequately enough. She recognised that, she even smiled, and said she understood. So perhaps it was labouring the point too much to go on and say what she did.

'So long as Ray's okay I can put up with all the blame. I know what I did shocked everyone rigid. Sister Tutor even hinted that I was . . . *am* far too friendly with him. Are we living in the Dark Ages? Are we supposed to nurse patients as though we *and* they are robots—never talking, never smiling, just clanking and planking on?'

His hand left her shoulder, he moved back to the desk and lodged on the edge of it, palms flat on its surface, feet firmly down on the floor. 'You're being a little extreme, surely? You must know what Sister meant. Friendship between a male patient and his nurse is always viewed askance. And Gilbertson makes no secret of the fact that he likes having you around.'

'We've a lot in common—the same sort of back-ground. Naturally we get on,' explained Anne.

'Yes . . . well, I don't make the rules, but we all have to stick by them. If you're so keen on talking to him why not do so as a visitor, during evening visiting, when you're off duty? No one could criticise then.'

'He's suggested that.'

'There you are, then.'

'I still think the rules are a pain,' she insisted.

'In that case . . .' he shrugged, and got up, went forward and opened the door, 'in that case I'm afraid you may have chosen the wrong profession.' He smiled, but hostility lay between them, cold and hard as a sword. 'Thank you again for your help just now.' His remark was politeness itself. It was also dismissive. Anne said goodnight and left.

She saw Ray Gilbertson during evening visiting twice before he went home. On the second occasion she met his employer, Mr Harold Lowe, who drove in from Dowford, a distance of eighteen miles. 'You must come and see us, once Ray's discharged,' he told her, shaking her hand. He was a big leonine type of man, he was lion-coloured as well. His hair, beard, skin and clothes were all the same yellowish fawn. 'It's nice for you two Aussies to meet.' He blinked tawny eyes at Anne.

'I was born in England, so that makes me English, but of course I know what you mean,' Anne said equably, smiling across at Ray.

'I can remember you emigrating, or rather I can remember Mrs Pentrose telling me about it the year we met at Crufts.' Harold Lowe stretched his knee and gave it a little rub. 'She didn't like it, didn't like it at all . . . not that she said a great deal. Plucky little woman . . . got more than her fair share of guts. Terrible for her, dreadful thing, losing her son in those fires.'

Ray's eyes went to Anne, who was staring at the wall. He knew about her parents, for Harold had told him last week, when Anne's name had cropped up in their talk, and since then he himself had touched on it with Anne. She seemed inured to the situation, but all the same, he felt, it was hardly the epitome of tact on the part of old Harry to mention her father as though his death was only the grandmother's loss. Ray wished he would get up and take himself off, but he didn't; he stayed for an hour. It was nearly the finish of visiting time when he finally took his leave, cramming a tweed hat on to his thatch of pale fawn hair, looking at Anne with approval, and saying, 'Well done!'

'He says that to everyone, quadrupeds included, can't break the habit,' said Ray. 'I'm so glad you sat him out.'

'I meant to do that,' she smiled.

He leaned forward and kissed her. 'You're a super girl, exactly the kind I like.'

'I'm glad to hear it!' She kissed him back, which wasn't difficult. His lips were fresh and didn't insist, his hazel eyes looked into hers.

'It's the first time we've done that.'

'So it is.' Anne sat back on her chair.

'It's a kind of hurdle . . . the first embrace.'

'Most first times are hurdles, Ray.' And some hurdles were insurmountable. With a jolt she thought of Charles.

'I wanted to kiss you,' Ray was saying, 'the very first time I saw you, when you were sitting exactly where you are now, frowning over some papers. We *are* going to meet, aren't we, once I get out of here?'

'You won't feel like going out in the evenings, not for a little while. And remember, I live here in London.'

'Not all the time you don't. Windon is only three miles from Dowford, you told me that yourself. When will your next days off be?'

'I don't think they're rostered yet. I've got one day off on the third of December, and I expect I'll go home for that, probably on the Friday night. I know Nella wants me to.' Anne turned her head sharply as the bell rang for the end of visiting time. Ray groaned and looked exasperated. 'I'll have to go,' she said.

'But we *will* meet?' He caught at her arm.

'Yes, of course we will.' She bent and kissed him, she even tucked him in.

He was discharged two days later. Mrs. Lowe came to fetch him. Anne saw him off, and saw him, too, for the first time in ordinary clothes . . . jeans, shirt, pullover, anorak . . . padded, and blue and zipped, right up to his chin, making his face look just a little fuller, making his hair look just a shade too long. 'I'll be in touch.' He squeezed her hand, then walked up the corridor, carrying his case which he'd taken from Mrs Lowe. He turned at the door and waved just once before he got into the lift. Anne entered the side ward and began to strip his bed.

It had been a very busy week, with three new admissions, and four discharges—the last one being Ray. The changeover of patients took some getting used to. It sometimes gave Anne quite a shock to walk into the ward, and see new faces and forms in beds which, hitherto, had been occupied by patients she had grown accustomed to over the weeks. She missed the complaining Mr Stevens, who had been transferred to Cardiac and, according to all reports, was doing well.

The youngest patient was an asthmatic—a sixteen-year-old boy. The Professor was carrying out various tests to try to discover the cause of his frequent attacks which had seemed to come, as the boy himself said, 'out of the blue, and I can't understand it, sir.'

There was a deaf patient with emphysema—a chronic disease of the lungs, which made expiration difficult. It wasn't easy for the nurses to deal with a stone-deaf patient. They had to write everything down on a pad, and put it in front of him. He would usually nod or shake his head; it was too much effort to speak, although he did so sometimes, in a hollow and strange-sounding voice.

The third new patient was a bus driver with a sudden

and painful attack of acute rheumatoid arthritis. He was febrile and very ill. He was being nursed on a firm mattress, and some of his joints had been splinted. He was virtually helpless, and a heavy nursing case.

So all in all there was little let-up, not that Anne minded that. There was plenty of scope for learning, with so much variety. As Charles Farne had told her, a medical ward was a good one to start on. Sometimes she felt she'd been on Livingstone Ward for years and years. She hadn't seen Dr Farne to speak to over the last few days. Once she had seen him at the entrance to Women's Medical with Leda. They were laughing over a toy giraffe that one of the patients had made. Two of the men in Livingstone were making stuffed toys at the moment—both under Leda's tuition, of course. They were getting them done for Christmas—now only four short weeks away.

Anne had heard from Ray. He telephoned her at the Nurses' Home. He said he felt good—Australian for well. He was working half-days in the surgery, finding it difficult with his sling, but leaving it off on occasion. He was driving again, he felt all right, and he badly wanted to see her. 'If you're coming home on Friday night, I'll pick you up early next day. I don't work on Saturdays, I shall have the car, we can drive off into the blue. What do you say? Don't you dare turn me down!'

'I wasn't going to,' his enthusiasm was infectious and flattering, 'but as for driving off into the blue, it'll be more like into the grey, or even the white . . . there's been snow in Scotland; we might easily get it here.'

'So I heard on the radio. Snow on high ground, it said. Well, that'll be an experience for me, never having seen the stuff.'

They talked for a few more minutes. It was good to hear his voice. And he sounds far more Australian over the telephone than off, Anne thought, as she replaced the receiver at last.

It was very cold on Friday evening when, with overnight bag in hand, she left the Nurses' Home and crossed the road. It wasn't snowing, but the rain that fell was interspersed with ice. She supposed it was hail, it pelted and bounced on her yellow mackintosh. No one, she muttered, could possibly, not possibly, like this. She had a long walk in front of her too, to Bank Underground, where she'd get the Northern Line to King's Cross, then a train to Dowford, and a bus to Windon. She sighed and wished she was there. She soon found she wasn't dressed properly; the fetching waterproof hat that matched her mac wasn't made for wind and hail; the brim either flapped down and blinded her, or blew up and nearly took off. Why was it that she always had such trouble with her hats? She was walking sideways, ducking her head, when a cream Mercedes car stopped at the kerb, and she saw Charles Farne through his rain-spotted window, leaning across to open the passenger door.

'Get in . . . look sharp!'

Anne dived in, hat, and bag, and all. She collapsed in a streaming heap on the seat, hearing the hail hit the roof. 'Oh, thank you . . . good of you . . . terrible weather!' She turned back the brim of her hat.

'I'm glad I saw you,' said Charles. 'I spotted you first as you left the Nurses' Home. I was turning out of the main gates then, and couldn't manage to stop.'

'Oh well, I hadn't got very far.' She looked at him and laughed, dabbing her face with a tissue, while he sat there dry as a bone in his tweed suit and polo-necked sweater, resting his hands on the wheel.

'Where are you going? Can I drop you off?' He glanced at her overnight bag. 'Put that in the back, if you like, and why not get rid of this?' His hand moved to the top of her hat and he lifted it off her head, like taking the lid off a saucepan. 'It was making you even more wet,' he explained with a smile, watching her shake back her hair. He was right, of course, but he had a nerve! 'So, where to?' he repeated. 'The nearest Tube or mainline station?'

'Bank, if that's all right. I'm making for King's Cross, I'm on my way to Dowford.'

'Dowford?' He looked blank-faced.

'I live there, or very near . . . at Windon, three miles out, with Nella, my grandmother.'

'Of course . . . of *course*, I remember now. I thought . . .' but what he had thought he declined to tell; instead he said, taking her breath away, 'I'll take you all the way there . . . no problem, as it happens.'

'But . . . *all* the way?'

'I'm going home too, to my parents at Seftonbridge. I go through Dowford, so it won't be too onerous a task to branch off and do the three miles along to Windon.'

'Well . . . if you're sure,' Anne said hesitantly.

'I'm perfectly sure.' He was drawing away from the kerb, rejoining the traffic stream, frowning over the wheel. When they reached the first set of traffic lights he switched the radio on. It was six o'clock, and the news was starting, the newsreader's voice filled the car, dispelling some of the tête-à-tête atmosphere. Sitting there listening to the spate of words, Anne began to relax. She also began to realise just what it was she had been spared—a beastly wet walk along to Bank, sardining on the Tube, probably a queue at King's Cross or, at best, a terrible scrum, for not only was it Friday night, but the rush hour as well. So, as Pru would say, thanks a bunch, she thought. Charles Farne could be very kind. He could easily have decided not to see her, and driven by with a swish. She stared out at the pelt of traffic, at the dazzling reflection of lights, at the windscreen wipers moving soundlessly, busily, on the glass, at the sleety rain which showed up in the beam of the headlamps like a stream of minnows falling down to earth.

They talked in snatches only till they got beyond Mill Hill. A financial talk followed the news, and Charles switched it off. 'If you want some music, twiddle the knob, see what you can find.' His hand went back to the steering wheel and he began to pass a van.

'I won't bother, thank you,' she said, 'it might send me off to sleep.' And that was a lie, if ever there was one, for she knew she would never sleep, not with Charles Farne sitting beside her, in sealed and close proximity. What a waste it would be to go to sleep, and oh, what a good thing it was that he wasn't psychic, and couldn't read her thoughts!

They spoke for a time about the new patients, especially about John Filton, the asthmatic boy, whose tests, so far, had all been negative. 'I'm pretty sure his attacks have a psychological cause,' said Charles. 'His parents are splitting up, you know—I gleaned that from the mother. John's a sensitive lad and attached to them both. I just hope they know what they're doing. There's little I can do in the matter. I doubt if they'll stay together simply to cure their son's asthma, they'll look to us for that. All we can do is dish out drugs, give him hope and confidence, and hope that in time he accepts the position . . . which he may or may not do.'

'Perhaps as he grows up and understands better. Sixteen is a vulnerable age.'

'One can be vulnerable at any age, more's the pity,' said Charles, and sounded so abrupt and angry that Anne was silent again.

It was when they were passing Lessitor Airfield and dropping down into Dowford that he asked her if she had heard from Ray. 'Do you know how Gilbertson is? He comes from Dowford, I seem to recall.' His tone was a little offhand.

'He does, and yes, I know how he is. He telephoned me at the Home. He's fine, working again part-time, sounded on top of the world.'

'Well, that's something.'

'It's a very great deal.' Anne tried to change the subject. Talk about Ray, perhaps because of the incident of his arm, and all the altercation that had followed, made an element of strain stiffen their conversation which, up to now, had been easy. She rubbed her hand over the passenger window and peered out into the darkness. It wouldn't be very long now before they turned off for Windon. It was still sleeting, but not so heavily, it was more like a sifting rain. 'Here's the signpost, this is where we turn.'

'Ah yes, now I'm in your hands.' Charles slowed for the corner, and they drove down a road not very much more than a lane. She wondered if she should ask him in, once they got to Litchfield Cottage. Nella would make him welcome, and a drink, or a cup of coffee and a sandwich maybe, would help him on his way.

'How long will it take you to get to Seftonbridge?' she asked.

'In these conditions . . . wet roads, darkness . . . about two hours,' he said. 'My father's not in the best of health, which is why I'm going just now. Normally I'd wait for a long weekend, or until Dr Cleaver's back. You've not met Susan Cleaver, have you?' Anne felt his eyes on her face. 'She's our house doctor, doing her year's internship. She's married to a GP in Hackney. She's on maternity leave at present, but is due back in a month, or a little less, the end of December, which will be a great relief.'

'Ellen Tillot told me about her. She said she was very well liked.'

'She is. She's been missed . . . certainly by me. Life's easier when Susan's around. She's the doctor mostly on call, the one who gets dragged out of bed at dead of night, or crack of dawn, poor girl.'

'Does it happen often?' asked Anne.

'Often enough.' Charles slowed as they came to the village. Once past the church she began to direct him to Litchfield Cottage, which stood at the end of a road called West Farm Lane.

It was in darkness, not the lane, but the cottage; there wasn't one lit-up window. It just stood there, solid and hunched, black and rectangular, chimneys blurred against the sodden sky. Anne stared at it in disbelief, as she got out on the verge. Nella always switched the lights on downstairs the second darkness fell, *and* the ones on the landing, *and* the lamp by the gate. She must have gone out, but how strange, she thought, when she knew I was coming home.

'Anything wrong?' Charles had joined her, he intended to see her inside.

'There aren't any lights—I can't understand it!' Anne fumbled with the gate, it droned back, and she went quickly up the path. She was nearly to the front door, Charles keeping pace beside her, when she realised with a pang of alarm that the dogs weren't barking . . . *they weren't barking* . . . they hadn't so much as yapped. 'The dogs aren't barking!'

He heard the alarm, even panic in her voice. 'But surely that means your grandmother's out, and has taken the dogs with her?'

'But she wouldn't be out . . . not now, at this hour. She takes them out at three, and gets back at four . . . or she does in the winter; she never varies the time. And she'd never take them out in the wet, they're stud dogs, they're valuable.'

'She might be with friends.'

'Well . . . she might, but I don't . . .'

'Let me have the key. We'll go in and see, that'll settle it. I expect she's left you a note.'

There was no note, but Nella had left a tea-tray set in the kitchen—a tea-tray obviously meant for herself, milk and sugar in the cup, tea-pot warming on the Aga, a buttered scone on a plate. 'It's her four o'clock tray . . . she meant to be back!' Anne rushed to the sitting-room. A brass guard shielded a fire that no longer had need of it . . . it had sunk down low and was very nearly out. The room was warm, the whole cottage was warm from the modern central heating. The droning sound of the pump working, and the splashing of rain in the gutters, were the only sounds to be heard as Anne ran from room to room—up the stairs, and back again, through into the annexe. 'Her mackintosh and boots have gone, so have the dogs' leads!' She pulled a telephone directory out from a set of shelves in the hall. 'I'll have to ring round . . . there are three people, friends she might have gone to! I'll have to make sure . . . I ought to find out!' She dialled the first number. There was no reply, so she dialled the second, and Mrs Harriet Tenant, a friend of Nella's who was arthritic, said no, she wasn't there. 'She never calls at this time, dear.' Anne thanked her and rang off. She dialled the third house and was told the same; she dialled Mr Grainger, the vet. His son said he'd seen Mrs P. with all six dogs, passing the surgery window just after three o'clock. 'It was fine then, but I remember thinking, good job she's well wrapped up.'

'You don't . . . didn't notice which way she went?'

'I'm afraid I didn't, no. She just passed, that's all. I didn't really think any more about it. Isn't it a little early to be worried? It's only half-seven, you know. She might have stopped off with friends when it rained. That'll be the answer, I'm sure.'

'Yes, maybe.' Anne couldn't argue, she couldn't stop to argue. She replaced the receiver and turned a blanched face to Charles. 'Something's happened to her! Something's wrong, I know it. She's fallen, perhaps, and is lying injured, or she may have been . . . attacked.'

There was a brief, leaping second while they stared at one another, joined by the words Anne had made herself say, and Charles felt the touch of her fear as chillingly as if it were his own. Its effect on him was galvanic; he knew what they had to do. 'Which route does she usually take? Which way does she go? Has she any special, favourite walk? Can you give me any clue?'

'I'm not sure . . . I don't know,' she struggled to think. 'She has several favourite walks, but today, with a wind, and if she thought it might rain, she could have gone through the woods. It'd be more sheltered, she'd go down the street and turn up Green Fan Road, into the woods, and down by the bridle path home.'

'Good . . . right, that's something to go on. Do you think you can find a torch, a good thick blanket too, we'll roll it and take it with us. We'll go in the car as far as we can, leave it, and walk through the woods. If she's there we'll find her.'

'And if we don't?'

'Then we'll have to tell the police. Come on, now, get that blanket and torch, I'll go and turn the car.'

Anne felt the swift pressure of his arm round her shoulders before he turned to the door, opened it, let in a gust of cold air, slammed it to behind him and ran down the path; she could hear the thud of his feet.

What would I do if he weren't here? Whatever would I do? She tore up the stairs to the airing cupboard, found a blanket and rolled it up. She searched for a torch; she thought there ought to be one in Nella's bedroom. Yes, here it was, a long, strong one, down by her bedside table. How many times had she heard Nella say: 'If a burglar gets in this house, he'll never know what hit him!' and she'd brandished the torch like a cosh.

Had someone attacked her this afternoon when she was out on her walk? Had she been mugged, had she been injured, had the dogs been stolen? They were valuable dogs . . . perhaps she'd been mugged, and the dogs had been taken away . . .

But I can't, mustn't think of that. We're going out to find her. We must find her . . . we have got to find her. Oh, please let her be all right! Charles started the car the second she climbed into it beside him.

And once more they drove off into the night.

CHAPTER SIX

THE rain was turning to snow as they drove down the village street to Green Fan Road and left the car on the verge. There was a short treeless incline before the woods began—a dark eyebrow running over the hill.

Charles carried the blanket, Anne the torch, and he grasped her other hand, as they made their way quickly through the trees. The torch cast shadows—sometimes their own; his shadow loomed beside hers. He looked bulky in a sheepskin jacket that he had had in the back of the car, and been thankful for when they had turned out into the cold.

The trees creaked, groaned, sighed, the wind rattled frozen branches; rain, or snow, or a mixture of both, dripped through partial clearings. They had been walking for nearly five minutes when they heard another sound, or Anne did, and she stopped Charles, jerking at his hand. 'Listen—stop! I'm sure I heard . . .' Both of them strained their ears, and then, above the weather sounds, faintly a short way ahead, they heard a crying, whimpering noise—an animal, a dog? 'Charles, it's them! It's one of the dogs!' She broke free and ran forward. 'Jolly! Jolly! *Jolly*! Here, boy!' and the whimpering changed to barking . . . a single raucous bark at first, then a volley, a storm of barks . . . several dogs . . . *all* the dogs. Anne ran towards the sound. Charles crashed behind her, and round the next bend, picked out by the torch, they saw the figure of a small woman lying prone on the ground. It was Nella, completely motionless, both arms out at full stretch, holding a lead in each of her hands; while on the end of each lead were three little spaniels, going wild with joy.

Anne rushed to and through them and flung herself down beside Nella. 'Darling, what is it . . . what's happened to you?'

'Fell . . . tripped. Anne, take dogs . . . don't let the dogs go loose.'

'Uncurl your fingers, give me the leads.' She tied them to a stump. Charles knelt by Nella. 'She's gone unconscious, probably just as well.' She watched his hands pass gently, skilfully over her grandmother's body, touching every part of it, reaching under her mac. The light from the torch made his face look hawked, his hair a curly crest. 'I can only guess, but I'm fairly sure she's got a fractured femur. I'll get an ambulance, they'll bring a stretcher, but while she's still unconscious we'll roll her very, very carefully over on to this.' He took off his jacket and laid it fleece side up on the rutty ground. 'Then we'll tuck the blanket round her, pray she'll retain some heat. Put your hands on her legs, high up . . . that's right . . . hold them firmly together. Now, over we go—that's it, that's fine.' Nella's face rolled to the sky; she gave a small moan, and as her eyes opened they stared straight into Charles'.

'I fell . . . hip broken, I think.' Her voice was stronger this time. 'Dogs lay on top, kept me warm . . . only got off when you came.'

'Mrs Pentrose, I'm a doctor,' said Charles. 'I'm going to get help. Anne will stay with you. I want you to lie as still as you possibly can.'

'Know . . . about that . . . was a nurse once.' The travesty of a smile moved her face which was pinched and drawn, while the tip of her nose showed the prominence of a patient suffering from shock. If she dies it'll be

from that, Anne thought . . . and she's no longer young.
Through a blur she saw Charles getting up. The dogs got
restive again. 'There's an ambulance station at Dowford,' he said, 'I'll ring from the nearest box . . . be
minutes only. You'll be all right, won't you?' He
touched the top of her head.

'Of course I will.' She watched him go. She had made
him take the torch, and the light bobbed up and down as
he ran, the dogs barked in noisy chorus. She untied
them, and they lay around Nella, pressing close to her
blanket—all except Jolly, who chose Anne's lap, and
promptly went to sleep. The comforting weight and
warmth of his body made her realise that six dogs lying
on Nella after she had tripped and fallen might have
saved her . . . might *still* save her from dying of damp
and cold. Sitting as close to her as she could, Anne began
to talk. She began to tell her how frightened they had
been when they hadn't found her at home. It seemed
necessary to talk, somehow . . . surely to talk was best.
Surely it was best to keep Nella as near to the surface as
possible, not let her lapse into deep unconsciousness.
She didn't seem to be in pain, or if she was she didn't say.
She wasn't really all that distressed; she even asked one
or two questions.

'Who did you say that young man was?'

'Charles Farne . . . Dr Farne, the one from the
hospital.'

'Oh, *that* one . . . but what was he doing . . .' Her
voice began to trail off. Under the blanket Anne felt for
her pulse. It was rapid, but easy to find; it wasn't
thready, nor especially feeble; perhaps she would be all
right. But hurry, Charles . . . oh, hurry, hurry! She
eased her cramped legs. Jolly protested at being disturbed—and then faintly in the distance, far, far away,
or so it seemed, she heard the wail of an ambulance. The

sound strengthened, the dogs alerted; sirens always made them howl . . . they howled now, and the mournful sound rekindled Anne's fears that her grandmother was about to die. Again she felt for her pulse. It was still beating, still beating . . . and the ambulance was coming. It had reached the village, the wailing siren stopped. Help was on its way, the men were coming, twigs crunched under their feet. Charles was leading, and the light they carried was like a searchlight beam. It illuminated the path through the woods in a harsh white brilliance; it picked out Anne and Nella, and the dogs—the latter barking furiously, Anne on her feet, shielding her eyes from the glare.

It was a mixed procession going back—Nella on the stretcher, an ambulanceman at each end of it, Charles at the side, Anne at the rear, holding the dogs on their leads. 'I'd like to go with her, in the ambulance, but I can't . . . not with the dogs.' She whispered the words, Nella's eyes were closed, but Anne knew she was semiconscious. She also knew that her greatest worry would be for her animals.

'Of course you can.' Charles fell back a pace and walked at the rear with Anne. 'You go with Mrs Pentrose, I'll take the dogs home in the car. I'll wait there at Litchfield Cottage until you ring . . . if I may. I wondered, earlier on, if you'd want . . .'

'But you've got miles of journey . . . all the way to Seftonbridge, and in this weather too! The local hospital may not keep Nella, they may transfer her on. I'd have to go with her, wherever it was, and it might take simply ages.'

'She's going to the Walbrook—I've arranged it, they're expecting her in Cas. Dowford Cottage Hospital is all right in its way, but they haven't the staff nor the facilities for dealing with orthopaedics. I thought it would save delay to get your grandmother straight to the Walbrook.'

'To the Walbrook . . . oh, heavens, *yes*! Oh, what a relief that is! Oh, Charles, thank you . . . what would we have done if you hadn't been here to help? I can be near Nella all the time; she'll be in London *with* me! I just can't tell you how grateful I am.'

'It's my job,' he said shortly. He took the dogs from her, and she handed him the keys. By then they were going down the incline from the woods to the grass-verged road. The ambulance, its flash still turning, stood in front of Charles' car. A thin mist of snow was falling. 'But the roads are all right, praise be!' one of the ambulancemen said, as he opened his rear doors and slid Nella into the warm interior.

Anne got in beside her and the ambulance pulled away. Charles stowed the dogs into his car, where they ranged themselves on the back seat. He could see their faces all in a row, as he quickly reversed and turned, then drove back through the village to West Farm Lane.

The ambulance reached the Walbrook just after nine, and Nella was taken through to the Accident Ward. She was X-rayed, put on a drip, and given an analgesic. To Anne's surprise, Mr Travers-Bentick, the orthopaedic consultant, came down to see her, once she was settled in. 'I was in the building, as it happened,' he said, 'when Farne's call came through. Now, I've seen your X-ray, Mrs Pentrose, and can tell you straightaway that you've fractured the neck of your femur, which means an operation. I'll do it for you myself tomorrow . . . leave you in peace tonight, allow you to rest to get over the shock, although I have to say you're in very good shape after all you've been through, very good shape indeed.' Nella just nodded; she wanted to sleep, she was very, very tired. Mr Travers-Bentick resembled a parrot with his high domed forehead and his large nose, polished, like a beak. She heard him ask Anne who she was, and she roused herself to tell him:

'She's my granddaughter, my next of kin, and my nearest and dearest; she's also a nurse, so you can tell her anything.' And now I can close my eyes and let them get on with it, she thought. She felt Anne squeeze her hand. 'Go home, child,' she said.

'Soon, darling—you go to sleep.' Anne walked back through the cubicles with Mr Travers-Bentick and listened to what he said.

'There's a degree of traumatic shock, of course—no use denying that. I prefer to wait till tomorrow before I operate. I shall reduce the fracture by internal fixation, nail and plate method. Afterwards she'll go up to Orthopaedics, and if all proceeds as it should, she'll be walking around the ward on a zimmer after fourteen days.'

'I'm glad she's under your care.' Anne spoke with a touch of awe, for even she had heard about Mr Travers-Bentick, the dedicated surgeon, who didn't spare himself, and who worked all hours, including Saturdays. She very nearly mentioned this, then decided not to; he might think she was being impertinent.

It was nearly ten o'clock when she left the hospital. A light snow was falling, with no diluting rain. She hadn't telephoned Charles yet, she would do so from King's Cross, tell him she was on her way; he would want to start off on his journey. She wished she had rung him earlier; he had put himself out so much, and then to keep him hanging about all this time was the absolute limit. There had been so much to do, though, to get Nella settled in . . . questions to answer, forms to fill in, a trip to the Nurses' Home to get toilet things, and the time had raced by, and now it was nearly ten. Anne was starting past the main gates when she saw Pru and Tom.

They were running down Farringdon Street, swinging hands and laughing, holding their faces up to the swirling snow. Seeing them, Anne had a sudden idea . . . perhaps Pru could help. She began to run to catch them up, calling as she did so: 'Pru . . . Tom . . . hold on! Please wait!'

They turned and looked at her—Pru in amazement. 'I thought you'd gone home!' she exclaimed.

'I had, but now I'm back, and now I'm going off again. Pru, listen, I want to ask . . .' Anne explained what had happened, walking along as she did so. There was no time to spare; whatever happened she mustn't miss her train.

'Oh, gosh, Anne, how awful!' exclaimed Pru, her round face berry red, white muffler flying back, Tom puffing beside her.

'So could you possibly do me a favour and ring my home number? Charles is still there, waiting to go. Tell him I'm on my way, tell him I'm getting the half-ten fast train from King's Cross. And tell him I'm sorry I've held him up. Will you do that, Pru?'

'Sure thing . . . yes, of course!' Pru and Tom were turning back. 'I'll ring from Cade House *now*,' yelled Pru. She couldn't get over the fact that Dr Farne was at Anne's home. 'However does she *do* it?' she remarked to Tom, as they dived across the road.

In the train, which she caught by seconds only, Anne sought to resolve her problems. There would have to be someone at Litchfield Cottage during Nella's stay at the Walbrook. The dogs couldn't be left unattended, they needed care and attention—feeding, grooming, exercising . . . and Queenie was heavily pregnant. Her litter was due in three weeks' time, she needed special care. Who would give it? Who can I get? 'Where on earth am I going to find it?' said Anne out loud, causing the elderly gentleman in the next seat to beg her pardon, and ask her what she had lost.

She still hadn't reached any solution when she got out at Dowford. She was going to get a taxi, she was too tired to wait for a bus—perhaps not so much tired as agitated, she couldn't endure to wait. If she couldn't get a taxi she would walk home; three miles wasn't far, except that it was bitterly cold; it was worse here than in London. The station was drippy, wet and windy; people were huddling and shuddering as they trudged over the iron bridge to give their tickets up. It's surprising the number of people who come home on the late train, passed through her mind just as she spotted Charles at the foot of the steps. He was looking up, he had seen her; he was wearing his sheepskin coat, his hands plunged deep in the pockets, and he was shifting and stamping his feet. He came forward to greet her, taking her by the arm.

'Good, you made it! How's Mrs Pentrose?'

'Not too bad, they're operating tomorrow. But, Charles, why haven't you gone? Didn't Pru tell you . . .'

'She gave me your message, but I seldom do what I'm told!' He gave her a lopsided smile as they passed through the ticket hall. 'My parents know I'll be late, I rang and told them so. I didn't much like the thought of you coming back late to an empty house. Besides, you must be tired out.'

'Bushed!' she said, and laughed; then: 'Thank you,' she added, glad to her very bones to have him there. An unusual shyness stopped her saying more.

'The dogs are all right,' he told her, 'they're lying in front of the fire. I made it up, made myself at home.'

'I'm very glad you did.'

'You've an in-whelp bitch, I see. How far on is she?'

'Six weeks. Queenie poses a problem, and I don't . . .' And then Anne stopped. She stopped and gasped, and stood and stared as they emerged from the station buildings. A white world met her eyes; snow lay thick on the trees, on the squat walls of the station surround, on the roofs of houses and shops, on sills and fences, the roads were mushy slush. 'Good Lord!' she exclaimed.

'Yes, I know—you can say that again! It's been coming down like this for the last twenty minutes.'

They crossed to the car, and she felt the flakes hit her face and melt. She heard the crisping, lisping sound they made as they hit her mac. It was nothing like the thin snow in town . . . this was the kind that meant business—the kind that laid, the kind that made a dozen Christmas card pictures, the kind that made havoc on the roads. 'You must have had a job getting here,' she commented, as they started off. Charles sat forward, peering over the wheel.

'It's a case of driving slowly, that's all.' They pulled out of the yard. The car in front had chains on its tyres, she could hear the sound they made. She knew Nella had chains in the garage; Charles ought to borrow them. Otherwise, how was he ever going to get to Sefton-bridge? He ought not to go . . . it isn't safe . . . it's far too dangerous, her thoughts ran on. Apart from that he needs to rest, I ought to ask him to stay. If Nella were here she'd insist on it. But it's got to come from me . . . he can hardly invite himself, can he? Yet still she hesitated. The going wasn't too bad in the High Street, but soon they were out of it, and forking on to the Windon road, which wasn't so trammelled by traffic. The car took it well, or perhaps it was just that Charles was a very good driver. Anne cleared a round of glass and stared out. The snow wasn't falling so thickly; she could just make out the top of West Farm Lane.

'Home safe and sound,' said Charles, starting to make the turn. And then, as though to prove him wrong, the big car slewed in a skid . . . a slow-motion skid, yet even so the sensation was paralysing. Anne had the feeling that her head and body were going different ways. She heard Charles' exclamation as the car continued to slide. His foot was off the accelerator and he was steering into the skid. After seconds only, which seemed like minutes, the wheels began to grip and revolve again; he managed to turn and point in the right direction. 'Hell, that was close!' he let out his breath. 'I thought we were bound for that ditch!'

'Charles, you can't drive to Seftonbridge, not tonight . . . it's far too risky!' Her words came out in the tumbling rush in the aftermath of the skid. 'You can't possibly drive all that way tonight. Please stay at the Cottage!'

'Well, thank you, I'd like to. I agree it's risky . . . in daylight it won't be so bad.'

'No, not nearly so bad,' Anne agreed. She sat back in relief. He had accepted the invitation so naturally. What had she worried about? Having cleared that hurdle (Ray's expression) she began to feel very much better. She began to plan supper, and where Charles would put the car. 'You can put the car in the garage with Nella's,' she went on easily. 'Hers is a small van, but there'll be plenty of room for both. As soon as we get in I'll heat up some soup, and see what else there is. You must be hungry.'

'So must you.'

'The last time I ate was midday,' she added.

'And now it's midnight . . . listen!' Above the hum of the car they could hear the church clock striking the hour, sounding flat and muffled, as though even bells were affected by the snow.

While Charles garaged the car, finding plenty of room alongside Nella's van, Anne trudged up the path and let herself into the house. The dogs gave her a rapturous welcome, she hugged each one in turn, then took them through to the annexe for the night. Jolly followed her back to the house, sticking close to her heels. He was puzzled and worried, he was missing Nella, he couldn't think where she was. Too many people he loved had gone missing from Jolly's life. Anne picked him up as she went to the sitting-room.

Charles was taking the guard from the fire. 'I won't make it up again, it's hardly worth it.' He gave the embers a poke.

'I agree, it's not.' She put Jolly down, and the little dog ran towards him, wagging his tail and half his body.

'So you,' said Charles, 'are the favoured one, who lives through in the house.'

'He does, yes. He's a pet, he's mine.' Feeling a shade embarrassed, Anne made her voice brisk; she looked at his case in the hall. 'If you like to bring that upstairs,' her voice was brisker still, 'I can show you round, show you which room you're in.'

'I can sleep down here—save work and trouble.' His eyes went to the settee.

'It's hardly trouble,' she said with a laugh, 'for me to make up a bed. I do it all the time, remember!'

'Yes, I suppose you do!' He laughed with her, but just for a second awareness flickered between them . . . awareness of the situation, a kind of realisation; her heart raced as she led the way up the steep narrow stairs, switching on the lights as she did so, talking all the time.

'There are four bedrooms—the cottage is rather bigger than you'd suppose. This is the one Nella usually likes to keep as the guestroom. It faces south, so you won't hear the wind, there's a bathroom leading off.' She opened a door on the right of the landing, moving swiftly before him into a square low-ceilinged room, tastefully furnished in cream, with twin beds, brocade curtains and a double radiator, turned full on and giving out comforting warmth. 'You may want to open the window for a minute—it's stuffy, isn't it?' She shot away from him, over to the window, and raised her arms to the sash.

'I'll see to that, *and* make my bed.' She felt his hands on her shoulders, gently but firmly moving her aside, then unsnibbing the window and moving it down to let in the icy air. With a brief glance at his Arran-sweatered back, she crossed to the airing cupboard, fetched sheets and blankets and laid them on one of the beds.

'I'll leave you to it . . . and find us some food,' she told him.

'Sounds marvellous,' he said. By then Anne was halfway down the stairs, and she nearly fell down the last two; she went into the kitchen and jerked the curtains across. Why on earth did she get into such a dither . . . why did this feeling creep in, spoiling the simple pleasure of his company, causing all this turmoil? Charles was completely unruffled and easy . . . don't let him guess how you feel. Half of it's probably due to the fact that I haven't eaten for hours. Away from him it seemed so easy to come to neat conclusions. She was perfectly calm, and the food was all ready by the time he came downstairs. He rang his parents, then sat down and did justice to the meal. Over it (they ate in the kitchen), he asked her about Jolly. She told him how he had been left in the house at Blandsyde during the two dreadful days of the fires. 'When Mother and Daddy failed to return, our neighbours let him out, and took him in with them, until I was able to get home. He nearly went mad when he saw me! I couldn't have left him behind . . . not when I came over here, I mean. I brought him back on the plane. After Heathrow I didn't see him, he had to go into quarantine. I was able to visit him every week; the kennels were in Essex. On the day I fetched him here to the Cottage we had a celebration. He's one of Nella's puppies, you know, so he's come back to his roots. Nella mated him with Queenie, so he's already earning his keep. I wish I could have him, but of course I can't, not at the Nurses' Home and he loves Nella, so it's best not to unsettle him again. The problem that faces me now is how to get the dogs looked after when I go back to London tomorrow. I racked my brains in the train, but didn't come up with any answer, apart from Mrs Thirle.'

'A neighbour?' queried Charles.

'No, Nella's cleaning lady. She comes most mornings. I'm sure she would stay here all day, and she wouldn't mind feeding the dogs, and cleaning them out, she's often done that . . . I know she'd help if she could. But I know she wouldn't stay overnight, she's got a husband and family. She'd have to leave here around five o'clock, and the night hours would be tricky.'

'The dogs can't be left?'

'They may have to be, but it wouldn't be ideal. They're valuable, and apart from that they're Nella's pride and joy. I simply wouldn't dare to tell her they were being left at night. I shall have to find someone from somewhere.'

'Would her vet help?' he asked.

'Mr Grainger?' Anne knitted her brows. 'Well, yes, he might, I suppose. I'll ring him tomorrow. He may know someone who would come and live in the house. I couldn't just have *anyone* . . . they would have to be recommended.'

'How about . . .' Charles reached for the butter, and helped himself to cheese, 'how about your Australian friend—our erstwhile pneumonia patient?'

'Ray is attached to another practice—to Mr Lowe's practice. He's the Dowford vet.'

'Ah, ethics again!'

Anne laid down her knife and fork. Deciding to ignore the teasing mockery in his voice, she answered him straightly, meeting his gaze head-on: 'I'm not quite sure what ethics prevail in veterinary practices, but if they're as rigid as hospital ones, then he wouldn't be able to come . . . not even if he wanted to,' she told him.

'True, very true.' His lashes flapped down. They were thick and silky and dark, yet as masculine as the rest of him. Even tired as he was, he still gave out a kind of strength and vitality and power that Anne had noticed the first time she had met him on the ward. Wilful, arrogant, stubborn, proud, she added inside her head. Yet how kind he could be . . . tender too. As he glanced up, she looked away. She half expected another remark couched in mocking tones. Instead she heard him ask her if she was home for the whole weekend.

'No, only for tonight. I intended to be here all day tomorrow, but as soon as I've rung Mrs Thirle I shall go up to town. I want to be near Nella—I want news of her first-hand. I hope they operate, I hope they plate her hip and get it done. I wonder how she is now. I wonder if she's all right. I suppose it's pointless to ring tonight?' Her glance moved over Charles' shoulder out into the hall where the telephone sat on its table. 'I suppose it wouldn't do very much good to give them a ring now?'

'It's twenty to one, and no, it certainly would not! Ring first thing tomorrow morning, that'll be much the best. And the best thing you can do for yourself,' his eyes raked her shadowed face, 'is to get to bed. I'll wash these up.' He moved over to the sink, bundling the plates and dishes in pell-mell.

'Oh no, Charles, I can't possibly let . . .'

'Don't be silly, of course you can.' He gushed torrents of water into the bowl, which splashed up from one of the plates, spurting over his sweater and into his face. He let out a stream of impressive oaths, grabbed the towel Anne passed him, but steadfastly refused to let her help.

He wasn't good at domestic chores, she noticed, with some amusement. In a way she found this rather endearing. She wondered if Leda did. One thought led to another, and she wondered what Leda would say if she knew where Charles was spending the night . . . not that she'd need to worry. Sighing a little—not entirely from tiredness—she locked up for the night, and when she saw Charles' back was turned she quickly and surreptitiously mopped up all the water he'd dripped on the floor.

They said good night on the landing with two doors between them, each smiling and thanking the other with polite formality. For all the world like hostess and guest, or landlady and lodger, Anne thought, brushing her hair with long, swinging strokes, before she finally tumbled into bed. I shan't sleep, passed through her mind . . . not so much as a wink. She was still thinking that five minutes later, but with slightly less conviction. The slide into sleep began then, the pace of the slide increased . . .

One could almost say she skidded down into the land of dreams, where Nella and Charles, and Ray, and the dogs, and the wail of an ambulance threaded in and out of her mind like a skein of silk.

CHAPTER SEVEN

THE milkman's float, and sounds from the hall, woke Anne at seven a.m. Sitting up in bed and straining her ears, she made out a man's voice—Charles' voice; he was speaking on the phone. Heavens, the phone . . . had it rung then? Was it the hospital . . . had something happened to Nella? She flung on a dressing-gown, opened the door, and began to descend the stairs.

The hall light was on and Charles was standing beneath it, replacing the phone on its cradle. He was fully dressed, spruce and brushed—he must have been up some time. 'Hello there,' he looked up and saw her. 'Did I wake you? I'm very sorry. I tried not to, but I thought you'd want early news of Mrs Pentrose. I crept down and made the call.'

'Is she all right? Has she had a good night?' asked Anne anxiously.

'So far, so good,' he said. 'I spoke to Sister, who says that Travers-Bentick is seeing her this morning. She feels fairly certain he'll go ahead and plate that hip of hers.'

'He said he would, if all went well.' She sat down rather quickly on the bottom stair, weak-kneed with relief. She passed her hands over and down her cheeks, looking up at Charles. 'She's practically my nearest relative, and closer to me than most,' she said, by way of explanation for her patently wobbly state.

'She'll come through with flying colours, Anne.' He bent and raised her up, holding her by the elbows, smiling down into her eyes. Her hair—long, thick, lustrous—curtained the sides of her face—a thin, finely-boned young face, pale and delicate-skinned. Her eyes, still cloudy with sleep, looked uncertain, her smile made him draw in his breath. He bent to Jolly, who was sniffing at his feet. 'I'll go and let him and the other dogs out, if you'd like me to,' he said. 'It's not late, it's not even light, not absolutely, that is. But I think I ought to be thinking of setting off fairly soon.'

'Oh, of course . . . yes. I'll go and get dressed. Has it snowed any more?'

'No, there's a bit of frost, though. Still, the roads should be all right. Yes, yes, I'm coming, you impatient little hound!' He unbolted the kitchen door and let Jolly out.

Anne showered and dressed at great speed, dragging on tights and sweater and cord dungarees, and tying her hair in a tail. She could hear the dogs in the orchard, and drawing back the curtains she saw Charles out there with them, ducking under branches loaded with snow which powdered down on his head. She saw him stoop and make a snowball and hurl it at a tree. He missed it, tried again and hit it. Target practice, she thought . . . and all men were little boys at heart. The dogs floundered back into their quarters, and he was trying his best to dry them when she went through to the annexe to see where he was. 'Towels,' she laughed, 'are superfluous. We've got a hot air system to dry them off, whenever they're damp or wet.' She showed him how it operated, pressing a switch on the wall. Hearing it click, the dogs all ranged themselves in front of the grid, closing their eyes in ecstasy at the warmth.

'Talk about luxury!' grinned Charles.

'Yes . . . well, it's a dog's life, so they say!'

'I'll be a canine, next time round!' He tucked his arm through hers. The important subject of breakfast was

mooted, and she learned that he didn't like eggs, nor was
he keen on bacon, not at this time of day.

'Toast, then . . . fruit and cereal?' She spread a cloth
on the table. 'Nella makes super marmalade . . . the
bitter, coarse-cut sort.' She sliced wholemeal bread,
tipped muesli into bowls, and set the coffee to perk while
Charles swept the snow from the paths, then came in
banging his hands. By then it was light, and the kitchen
was warm, redolent of coffee and toast, and the tang of
orange; the two of them sat down to eat.

In spite of niggling, unresolved worries, Anne felt in
better spirits. Charles was quiet, but even he seemed
more relaxed this morning. There was an easiness between them which hadn't been present last night. There
had been a need to chatter then; this morning that need
was dispelled. A feeling of companionship put paid to
banal talk. Perhaps this is what being married is like, she
thought, refilling his cup. He caught her eye. 'Penny for
them.'

'Sorry, I didn't quite catch . . .'

'Penny for your thoughts.'

She went bright pink. 'They're too way out to
divulge.'

'You disappoint me,' he drawled.

'Well, that's too bad.' She smiled and he looked at the
window, muttering something about getting out the car.

'I really ought to be making a move, but I'll help you
wash up first,' he said.

'That's kind, but no, there's no need. I'll do that when
you've gone, and start my ringing round as well to try to
enlist some aid . . . first Mrs Thirle, then Mr Grainger,
see what gives,' said Anne. She broke off then, chewing
her lip; she had just remembered Ray. He was coming
round *and* coming early, as that had been the plan. They
had been going to spend the day together, to drive off

into the blue. Ray was the main reason why she had come home last evening, but now, of course, everything had changed. She would have to ring him, to explain the position, for he might not want to turn out—not as she had to return to town so soon.

She watched the chassis of Charles' Mercedes emerging from the garage, its exhaust billowing misty fumes; he was turning to face the road. Anne thrust her feet into boots and went down the path to see him off. 'Don't get out again,' she called, trying to quicken her pace, making a slide on a hard patch of snow, which whisked her to the gate. He got out of the car and gathered her to him, swinging her round in an arc.

'Nurse Pentrose, making a *slide*!'

'Dr Farne, throwing *snowballs*!'

'You saw?'

'I did.'

'That makes us quits.' He stopped her laugh with a kiss, and her lips responded and moved with his, and the sparkling winter morning swam in a sea of white behind his head.

Anne's breath jerked. 'Safe journey,' she said, as he set her down at last. She put her hands on his arms, and he leaned forward and kissed her nose.

'You'll get cold, go back in.'

With an effort of will she moved away from him. She even managed to jest a little. 'Yes, Doctor,' she said. It was when she half turned to retrace her steps that she saw the green estate car crunching to a halt outside the gates. Charles saw it too.

'Hello, you seem to have got an early caller.' Then he stopped in his tracks and openly stared as the car door opened and a pair of long, blue-jeaned legs swung out.

'It's Ray. He said he'd be over early,' he heard Anne say behind him. And there was no need to introduce them, although she gained the impression that at first Ray couldn't quite decide who Charles was, then recognition dawned, and he held out his hand.

'Is someone ill?' His glance went beyond them to the open door of the house. 'Has there been . . . is anything wrong?' And again he asked it of Charles.

'The answer to that is "yes", I'm afraid. Anne will fill you in,' Charles said shortly, getting into his car. He kept the door open for a second or two, still speaking to Ray. 'It's good to see you again, Gilbertson, and looking remarkably fit, in spite of this seasonal weather . . . mind you keep it up.' He smiled the sort of smile he reserved for patients in the ward, then got into the car and slammed the door. He made as if to move off, then pushed the window down. 'How did you find the roads this morning? I've a fair journey to do.'

'The main ones fine, the side ones tricky, but the gritting machines are out.'

'That's something.' He looked at Anne, and Ray stood back on the path. He heard the two of them saying goodbye, heard something about 'hospitality' and 'getting all your arrangements made', and 'good news by this evening'. And then the Merc was moving off, steering past his estate car, and Anne was tugging him into the warmth of the house.

'Coffee first, there's plenty left. Take your anorak off, and sit here by the Aga.' She let the front of it down. Ray did as she said, but reminded her too, in a voice she well remembered, that he didn't want fussing, that he wasn't an invalid now.

'Where's Mrs Pentrose? Is it she who's ill?' He looked at the breakfast things, still on the table; he watched Anne reach for a cup.

'She's had an accident.' She sat down with him, pulling Jolly on to her lap. She told him all that had happened, starting from the moment when Charles had picked her up in his car, and ending with this morning, when he'd rung the Walbrook to see how Nella was. 'He's been so helpful . . . very supportive.'

Ray said how sorry he was. He sipped his coffee. 'But I wish I'd been here,' he added.

'You're here now, and I'm very glad.' Her eyes went to the clock.

'I thought you didn't like Farne very much, but still . . .' he put down his cup, 'I'm glad he helped, came in useful. He owed you something, didn't he, after all that furore about putting my shoulder back.'

'I don't think either of us thought of that . . . at least not consciously. You can't nurse a grievance for ever, can you?'

'I'm not the forgiving type,' said Ray with the ear-to-ear grin Anne remembered from the ward. His face had filled out since last Saturday (was it only last Saturday?) when he'd been discharged and gone home with Mrs Lowe. 'I'm so sorry about Mrs Pentrose,' his hazel eyes met Anne's green ones. 'How long will she be an in-patient? Who will you leave the dogs with? And which one are you?' He spoke to Jolly, who rounded his eyes in scrutiny, then fluttered his tail against Anne's dungarees.

She smiled. 'That means he approves of you. Jolly's mine, he's a special pet. The breeding dogs live in the annexe—I'll show you them in a minute. As to what I'll do, how I'll manage, that's anyone's guess at the moment. If all goes well,' she crossed her fingers behind Jolly's chestnut back, 'Nella should be home in roughly three weeks' time.'

'They're using the pinned method, then?'

'Nail and plate fixation. Then if she's pain-free and . . . and all right,' again she crossed her fingers, 'she'll be allowed to walk about, to bear weight on the limb, with the aid of a zimmer, once the sutures are out.'

'It's a hell of a problem—tough, isn't it?' Ray pushed back his slope of blond hair. 'Will your vet board the dogs?'

'Oh, *I* don't know.' Anne felt testy and worried again. 'Even if he would, I don't feel it's the proper thing to do. They ought to be kept in their own quarters. One of them's preggers, you know,' she explained about Queenie. 'She's only about sixteen days from her whelping time. I'm pinning all my hopes on Georgina—Nella's cleaning lady. If she'll agree to come and live here for three weeks, it would take care of everything. She'd have to call Mr Grainger in for Queenie's confinement, of course, but apart from that there'd be no problem. She's devoted to the dogs. She doesn't mind what she does for them in the way of cleaning out and grooming, etcetera.' She got up from her chair and cleared the table. 'Ray, I'm terribly sorry about today, but you do see how I'm placed? As soon as I can I must get back to Town. I want to be at the hospital when Nella comes out of theatre. I ought to have rung you last night.'

'You had other things to think about.' Ray put his arm round her waist. Anne didn't protest, nor pull away, but he felt her stiffen up. She kept her face well to the front too—he saw it through clouds of steam, as she washed the cups and bowls and plates he'd seen on the breakfast table. He wanted to ask her if she had slept with Farne, but decided not to risk it. There was something about the set of her head that warned him not to ask questions. Instead he took the gold tassel of hair hanging down her centre back and swung it gently, watching the end curl round the heel of his hand. 'Take me through to the annexe and I'll see to the dogs for you,' he said. 'I expect Queenie has a meal of sorts?'

'Yes, she does. I'll give you her diet. But, Ray, are you sure you want to be bothered?' Anne turned round, wiping her hands.

'Positive . . . couldn't be more so.'

'But in those clothes,' she said. She looked at his pale blue shirt and pullover, and brand new denim jeans, with a kind of vexation that made him want to laugh. 'My clothes *are* washable, Annie!'

'You can wear Nella's apron,' she told him.

'Oh, hey now . . . come *on*! I'm not a pinny man!'

'It's a man's apron, you'll not be in drag!' She found Nella's hessian treasure hanging by its strings from one of the pegs in the hall. When Ray saw it he agreed to put it on, and he followed her through to the annexe. It was when she had left him, when he was filling the five separate water bowls and giving Queenie her egg and milk, and enjoying the sight of the dogs, that the idea came to him; he sat back to think it out. On the face of it he could see no snags, providing the Lowes agreed, and providing Anne did, and also Mrs Pentrose.

Through in the hall, Anne was on the phone to Mrs Georgina Thirle, who promised, after a good deal of agitated squeaking, to help out in any way she could. 'But how shocking! Your poor dear grandma, she won't like being laid up. About two or three weeks, you say . . . well, yes, I could manage that. Not Sundays, though, I must have my Sundays, but on weekdays, yes, I'll come. I'll come along each day at nine and stay till half-past five. Tell your grandma not to worry, I'll see her and her doggies right.' She was so spontaneously willing that when it came to the crunch, Anne simply couldn't bring herself to ask if she'd stay all night. It wouldn't be right, she could see that, so she thanked Mrs Thirle who, after more squeaking and background consultation with her spouse, said she'd come along . . . 'at two o'clock this very day, Miss Pentrose. Might as well start as I mean to go on. Oh, your poor dear grandma . . . makes me go all funny to think of what she's been through!'

Anne put down the phone and let out her breath, then sinking down on the stairs, she rehearsed what she would say to William Grainger, the vet. She was just about to dial when Ray came through from the annexe.

'How are you getting on? Any luck?'

'With Mrs Thirle, yes.' She explained the arrangement. 'She's a decent sort, she's been with Nella for years. I didn't ask her to stay over at nights, I feel that's a man's job really. I was just about to ring Mr Grainger . . .'

'Anne, before you do,' Ray took off his apron and rolled it up, 'would you let me do it?'

'What, ring Mr Grainger?' she blinked at him.

'No, let me come and stay here . . . for the next three weeks, if Harold Lowe agrees.'

'Sleep here?' she queried.

'Yes, be here when Mrs Thirle's gone home. I'd need to tie up with Harold Lowe, but I don't think he'd object. I don't start morning surgery till nine, the evening one ends at six, and I've been let off night calls until I'm properly fit. I'm not complaining, but it's cramped at the Lowes' . . . here I could spread myself. I'd be able to study, catch up on my reading, and as for getting to work, three miles into Dowford is nothing; so how do you feel about it? Do you think your grandmother would mind?'

'No, I don't.' Anne was on her feet, relief washing over her. 'I'm quite sure she wouldn't, and as for me, I'm speechless, I really am! I didn't dare hope that you'd want to do it.'

'I do, very much indeed. I'll ring Harold now.' Ray reached for the telephone.

Five hours later, with arrangements complete, and with Mrs Thirle doing her shift, Ray drove Anne into Dowford to catch the London train. A wintry sun was bearing warmth, melting the snow to slush. 'There won't be much left by morning, I can't say I'm sorry,' said Ray, watching a slide of it gush off the station roof.

'Some people like it,' Anne replied, releasing her safety belt, and seeing again in her mind's eye a clear vision of Charles plunging about in the orchard, throwing snowballs at a tree, 'it holds a kind of enchantment for some.'

Ray shuddered. 'Not for me! In Perth, now, it'll be high summer. Don't you miss it at all?'

'Yes, sometimes,' she started to say, but there wasn't time to finish. The train was coming round the bend as they crossed the iron bridge; they could see its bright orange front, hear the haw of its diesel engine. And then they were rushing down the steps, up and along the platform. Anne got a seat in a non-smoker, then leaned out to speak to Ray. 'Thank you again. I can't tell you how pleased . . .' More people pushed into the carriage. 'Ray, don't wait, you'll only get cold!' A youth pushed the window up. Anne left it closed, signalling to Ray, who got the message at last and moved away, waving from the steps. He didn't like the English winter, but perhaps that wasn't surprising. The Australian climate, and life, was so different; she understood how he felt. The train began to pull out of the station, and she watched the red brick houses on the outskirts of Dowford flash by and pass from sight.

It was just on two o'clock when she reached the Nurses' Home. Stopping only to dump her things, she went across to the hospital, and up to Orthopaedics on level three.

Orthopaedics was a complete unit, not just a couple of wards. There were four wards, two operating theatres, a plaster theatre and X-Ray, a physio section, and ancillary rooms besides. A reception desk guarded the entrance, and a girl in green-rimmed glasses looked over it, and at Anne, in some surprise. 'It's not visiting for another hour.' (Anne was in 'civvy' clothes.)

'I know, but I'm not a visitor, as such. I'm a nurse in the hospital. I just want to know how my grandmother is—Mrs Fenella Pentrose. She had an operation this morning. Mr Travers-Bentick performed it . . . a fractured neck of femur.'

'Oh, *yes*!' A smile curved under the glasses. 'Mrs Pentrose is in Anderson Ward. I'll get Sister to speak to you.'

'She has had it . . . the operation, I mean?' Anne couldn't help feeling jumpy.

'Yes, she's been back in the ward some time, but I've not heard how she is. I shan't be a minute. Wait there, please.' The girl came back in record time with a positive giantess of a Sister—six foot three at least. She towered above the green-glasses girl, and her voice was as large as her frame.

'I'm Sister Beatty,' she informed Anne heartily, 'and you'll be Anne Pentrose. Your grandmother's come through very well, she's been round from the anaesthetic and she's sleeping naturally now. You can sit with her, if you like. She's unlikely to rouse, and even if she does she'll be muzzy and disorientated.'

'I understand that, but I'd like to see her.'

'Tomorrow she'll be compos mentis, more herself again, sitting up, maybe. Mr Travers-Bentick is pleased. Come along then, dear, this way.'

Anne walked past the desk, smiled at the girl, and followed Sister Beatty down the short passage leading to Anderson Ward. It seemed light, and enormous, and very full . . . overwhelming at first. She got a swift impression of pulleys and weights and plastered limbs, hoists, zimmers, and wheelchairs, and complicated frames. Nella was in the third bed down, her curtains had been pulled back. She was lying flat, with just one pillow, and a cradle over her legs. Her normally ruddy face was pasty, her hair tousled and rough. Her arms lay outside the coverlet, and she had a defenceless look—a vulnerable look, that made Anne's throat constrict. It was then that she realised—painfully realised—how very different it was to see someone one knew and loved looking ghastly ill in bed. To see *anyone* ill could be very disturbing, at least to a learner nurse, but to see a loved one looking like that was a chastening experience. And however much she told herself that Nella's deathly appearance was due to the general anaesthetic which hadn't yet worn off, she still felt torn; and in the end, after sitting and holding her hand for several minutes, she wanted to get up and go.

'Come tomorrow, dear, when you're off duty.' Sister came out of her room, filling its doorway with navy-blue and white. 'I'll leave word with staff nurse to let you go in any time you like.' She saw Anne out, right to the lifts, and pressed the button for her.

'For all the world,' Anne told Nurse Lyne next day on Livingstone Ward, 'as though I were a visiting VIP!'

'She's like that, she's got a name for it. Everyone likes Sister Beatty,' said Jane Lyne, with her eye on Ellen, who was taking old Mr Pride along to the day room for the Sunday service, which was just about to begin.

All the staff on the ward were sorry to hear about Nella's accident, but apart from Pru, Anne hadn't told anyone about Charles' rescue act. Facts were apt to get distorted, especially in hospitals. He might not want his part in it shouted from the rooftops, so she just said Nella had fallen, and left it at that.

She went down to see her at four-thirty, as soon as she was off duty. She went just as she was in uniform . . . dress and cap and cloak. A sight for sore eyes, if ever there was one, Nella thought as she saw her approach— tall, fair, straight and proud, my beautiful granddaughter. The two embraced, each feeling emotional.

'You're sitting up. Sister said you might be,' Anne brought a chair to the bed and sat down, slipping off her cloak.

'They get you humanised as quickly as possible. Oh, good, you've brought my things.' Nella was glad to see her own nighties, and dressing-gown, and toilet things. 'Good girl, you've thought of everything.'

'All due to my training,' said Anne, 'but how are you? Is your leg painful?'

'Sore, more than actually painful, but that'll be the stitches. I've had Angela Rivetts up to see me . . . your much esteemed SNO. Evidently Dr Farne, when he had me brought in here, said that I was a one-time colleague of the Senior Nursing Office. I suppose *you* told him that?'

'Yes, I did, several weeks ago.'

'I saw her in the summer, remember, before you started here? She's a nice woman . . . fourteen years my junior, but she never rubs that in. She's done well, shot right to the top of the tree, and she likes your Charles Farne, says he's a very caring doctor; she hopes he'll stay at the Walbrook, and further his career within these walls. Ask him to come and see me when he's got a minute, will you? I'd like to thank him for all he's done, and meet him properly. Now, about the dogs,' her main anxiety pushed itself to the fore, 'have you got Georgina Thirle to stay?'

Anne explained the arrangements she had made, while Nella leaned back on her pillows. She blinked a little when she heard about Ray's part in it all. 'I'd like to see this young man,' she said.

'You can, he's coming tomorrow. There's no official visiting on Mondays, but Sister will let him in. He realised you'd want to look him over.'

'Yes, well, that figures,' said Nella, using the Americanism which she had heard on Anne's lips often enough, and secretly deplored. 'Everyone's rallying round me, and I find that very heartening.' She tried to smile, but her lips were drooping and her mouth was going slack. She wanted to sleep, and Anne let her do so, taking her hand in hers. Sitting there on the bucket chair, she watched her grandmother's face, watched the pulse that beat in her throat above the hospital gown. She sat there until the bell rang for the end of visiting, then took her chair back to the table and left the ward.

When she returned to it on Monday she found Ray at Nella's bedside. They were chatting together like old friends, which portended well, she thought. Ray sprang to his feet at her approach and fetched another chair. 'I like him, I like his manner, and he knows what he's about,' said Nella in a sibilant whisper, just before he returned.

Her colour was better today, Anne noticed, she seemed more her old spry self. 'I was visited by Mr Travers-Bentick this morning, who told me I was a wonder, and ordered my suction drain to be removed,' she said with a grin. 'Now, what could be more cheering and complimentary than that?'

'I should imagine, not a thing!' laughed Anne.

'While Mr Gilbertson (Nella belonged to the old

school and tended to be formal) has been telling me about the dogs, who he says are missing me, but who've settled down, and decided to settle for *him*.'

'Yes, well, that shows what a fickle lot they are.'

'They're a fine healthy lot,' said Ray, 'and I must say I like the breed. They're game too—I swear they were sorry to see the last of the snow.'

'Which you weren't,' teased Anne.

'It's not my favourite stuff.'

'No, nor mine,' agreed Nella, 'but I expect we'll get some more. It's a recognised fact that England gets its worst weather after Christmas. And talking of Christmas, I intend to be home for it,' her look became defiant, 'even if I have to walk around on my hands!'

'I should think you'll be discharged by then—there are three and a half weeks to go. You might even make it before Queenie's pups are born.'

'She's not a maiden bitch, she's had a litter before, so there shouldn't be any problem with her,' Anne heard her say, but by then her attention had wandered, for just outside the ward doors she could see Charles Farne talking to Sister, see the two of them coming in.

'Another visitor, Mrs Pentrose!' Sister feigned annoyance. 'Two is the limit, even during regular visiting.' In a way she was joking, but making a point in the nicest possible way. One of us will have to go, Anne thought, watching Charles and Nella shaking hands and exchanging smiles, while Ray rose to his feet:

'Have my chair,' he said to Charles. 'It's time I went, anyway. I'll be back on Saturday, Mrs Pentrose. I don't have a clinic then.'

Feeling that the least she could do was walk with him to the doors, Anne got up and did so, half of her glad to escape, the other half . . . the weak half . . . rampaging to get back . . . to get back to Charles. And I must, she thought, be out of my tiny mind. What is it about him that makes me long to be independent of him, yet also, and even more strongly, makes me long to be where he is? What is it about him that pulls me to him, that makes me feel so helpless, that binds me to him with a kind of . . . potency?

She glanced back into the ward at him, as she stood with Ray in the passage. Amongst all the plastered legs and arms, the coverlets and pillows, his reddish-brown hair above his white collar made an impacting focal point. The lights were on, and his hair glowed, his face was turned towards Nella. 'You like him, don't you?' Ray followed her glance, and although the question shook her, she didn't dissemble, nor pretend not to know what he meant.

'I didn't at first, but now I do. I've got to know him better. He improves on acquaintance.' She tried a laugh that didn't quite come off. 'Why do you ask? Don't you like him? I think perhaps you should.'

'You mean because he did his job and got me well again? Oh, I admire him for that, I respect him for that, but liking's another thing. The doctor and the man are two things apart. As a man he's not easy to read, as a man he's deep, he guards his own secrets. At least, that's how I see him.'

'He's entitled!'

'Sure thing!' Ray bent and kissed her, his mouth pressuring hers with a bruising roughness that took her by surprise. 'I'll see you on Saturday. Until then, be good.' He went swiftly up the corridor, moving towards the reception desk, where the girl in green glasses sat. Anne went into the ward and joined Charles at Nella's bedside. The three-way talk that followed was mostly about Nella's fall. After that it veered to Christmas, and how it was celebrated in the wards and departments of

the Walbrook Hospital. Anne left when Charles did,
some ten minutes later. Nella had had enough. All she
wanted to do was lie there and think about her visitors,
and perhaps doze off for an hour or so before supper was
brought round. It was astonishing how tired she got . . .
still, it was early days yet. How nice that Anne had so
many friends, how appealing she had looked tonight.
The young man, Ray, was in love with her, couldn't take
his eyes off her face. I never attracted men like that, but I
got the one I loved, Nella thought. She fell asleep, and
dreamed about Jonathan Pentrose, the young doctor,
who had courted and won her, and died of a heart attack
fifteen years ago on Christmas Day.

Anne and Charles stood at the lifts, she straining to
make conversation. It was strange how the fact of her
being in uniform made talking to him so difficult. It was
the status thing, the chasm between—the wide, unspannable one. On his side he stood as the senior doctor,
on her side she stood as a nurse . . . a learner nurse, the
lowest form of life. In her sensitised state she felt the
difference, and felt that he maintained it . . . purposely;
he was affable, but aloof.

'Did you get home all right and . . . enjoy your
weekend?' Even to ask him that seemed out of place,
and over-friendly. He stood very straight at her side.

'I had no trouble,' he looked at the flicking numbers
above the lifts. 'I'm delighted about your grandmother,
and I know Travers-Bentick is.' He looked at her
then, and half-smiled, and courage came back with a
rush.

'Most of it, the good outcome, is due to you,' she said.
His Christian name very nearly came out, but she bit it
back in time. She ought to say 'Doctor', but she couldn't
say either; she couldn't say anything more.

'Glad to have been of service.' He was looking down

at the floor. 'Mrs Pentrose mentioned that Gilbertson's turned up trumps.'

'Yes, he has. It was such a relief. He came right out and offered.'

'Good for him, I'm glad to hear it,' he said, as the lift arrived, opening its doors, yawning empty; he stepped in and held it for her. 'I think I'll go up to the ward,' he added, 'so this is all yours.'

'Thank you.' Anne got it, and the closing doors cut him from sight.

It was silly to feel, as the lift bore her down, that he had purposely despatched her . . . not dismissed her exactly, but got her out of his way.

CHAPTER EIGHT

DURING the run-up to Christmas Nella continued to make good progress. On the tenth post-operative day her sutures were removed. Four days after that she was weight-bearing on the limb, walking up and down the ward with the aid of a zimmer, applauded by Mr Travers-Bentick himself. She was discharged on the twenty-second of December, much to her delight. Her sister from Warminster, who was staying with her till the end of January, was at the Cottage, as well as Mrs Thirle.

'So does the Aussie go back to his lodgings?' Ellen enquired next morning, when she and Anne were trimming the silver tree in Livingstone Ward.

'He does, yes.' Anne opened the steps and looked at the top of the tree. 'He doesn't say so, but I think he's had enough of the quiet life. It'll be swinging at the Lowes' over Christmas, with their son and daughter home.'

'Will you be with him for New Year?'

'He's going to Scotland then. He's got cousins there. Can you pass me that bell—the one on top of the box?' Ellen did so, and Anne hooked it on and stood back to see the effect. The tree—an artificial one—had been brought out of store yesterday. Fir trees, the genuine article, weren't allowed in the wards; they were reserved for the landings and hall and courtyard, where the scattering of their needles was less of a hazard to the cleaners and all concerned.

The big tree in the courtyard had been set down near

to the fountain. Its lights were switched on at dusk each day, when its stately dark-hued beauty took on the magic and mystery of Christmases long, long ago, when gas-lamps lit the London streets, and horse-drawn carriages took elegant crinolined ladies to parties and balls.

It had been in the courtyard for ten days now, and in Anne's eyes it vied in beauty with the big one from Norway that stood in Trafalgar Square. She and Ray had gone to Trafalgar Square last evening. They had sung carols with various groups, drunk coffee from a stall, and eaten roast chestnuts, and felt a part of it all. Ray hadn't once, at least not out loud, made comparisons with Perth. She had felt a deepening of affection for him, and had loved his Christmas gift of a pair of carved bookends in the shape of two King Charles spaniels. 'However did you find them . . . they're lovely, Ray!' She had put them back in their box.

'I looked till I did.' He was quiet for a while, then said in a kind of rush, 'I knew that anything rather more personal would be handed back to me.'

'These are perfect,' she'd said again, and they had gone out for their evening, which had proved to be their most successful yet.

'Here comes Doctor,' said Ellen, breaking into Anne's thoughts, and giving her—she noted with glee—the shock she'd fully intended, making her drop her tin of frosting spray. 'The female one, Dr Susan Cleaver.' She stopped and picked up the tin. 'She's come to see John Filton, I expect.'

'Yes, no doubt she has.' Anne's heartbeats returned to normal, as she quickly descended the steps. She had met Dr Cleaver a week ago, and liked her instantly. She was plump and jolly and open-hearted, with a round dimpled face, mouse-brown hair which was naturally curly, and cropped close like a boy's. She treated everyone alike. Status to Susan Cleaver was an unknown word; people were people so far as she was concerned.

No sooner had she got through the doors than she stopped to admire the tree. 'Someone's got an artistic touch,' she smiled at the two girls.

'Don't look at me, Doctor,' laughed Ellen, 'I don't know a bell from a bauble. Anne's directing operations, and a good job too.'

Ellen could be infuriating, but she could also be very generous, passed through Anne's mind, as she watched Susan Cleaver wave to Staff Nurse Lyne and make her way down the ward to see John Filton, the asthmatic boy. John was sitting by the side of his bed, doing a jigsaw puzzle on a large tray, which Sister had found for him. Whether Dr Cleaver's chats with John (and she had spent much time with him) had made him face up to the fact of his mother and father's split marriage, or whether his three weeks in hospital had lent a kind of balance— even, perhaps, a little maturity—was anybody's guess. The fact was that the boy's attacks were becoming far less frequent. He was off all steroids and tranquillisers, and a course of physiotherapy had taught him the special breathing exercises he had to start at once if he felt an asthmatic attack was imminent. He was being discharged on Friday, the day before Christmas Eve.

'To which parent?' Susan Cleaver asked him, looking him straight in the eye.

'To Dad. He's the one who needs me most. Mum will be with her boy-friend. I've met him, you know. She brought him with her yesterday afternoon. He gave me this,' he pointed to the puzzle, 'it's a rare old mix-up.' Whether he meant the jigsaw, or the domestic situation, Susan Cleaver had no idea, but the main thing was, he was no longer tearing himself to bits.

She saw one more patient, then left the ward, and met

Anne in the corridor. Anne was on her way to coffee, it was nearly half-past ten. Susan asked her if she had seen the decorations in Paediatrics. 'If you haven't, spare a minute to go—it brought all my childhood back. I'm going along there now, they hadn't quite finished it yesterday. Skip your coffee and come with me. You'll be thrilled, I know you will.'

'I'd love to, Doctor,' smiled Anne. So off they went to the children's wing, on the other side of the hospital, looking towards St Giles' Church, Cripplegate. The lift took them down, and they crossed the yard in the pale winter sunlight, stopping just briefly to admire the giant tree. Anne asked Susan how her baby was, and she told her he was fine. 'It's heaven having a tiny baby at Christmastime, you know. Simon's ten weeks old now, and growing by the hour. It's a real wrench to come to work and leave him with my mother. I expect I shall get used to it, but the tie is very strong, or it is at first; you feel they're still joined to you, in a way. You'll know what I mean by that when you have a child of your own. Well, here we are.' They entered the corridor leading down to the ward. Sister Mason waved them in, and Anne caught her breath at the scene.

Streamers and lanterns hung from the walls, every window-pane was frosted, every bed and cot had a different trimming, while at the far end, near the desk, were cardboard cut-outs from *The Wind in the Willows*—Badger, and Ratty, and Mole, not to mention Toad himself, set against wonderful scenery of Toad Hall with its crenellated towers. At the day room end was a tree and a crib, with animals gathered round, made by talented patients from various wards. The scenery behind the crib showed the three Wise Men, and the Angel Gabriel, looking a little surprised.

'Something went wrong with the face of the angel. I

could not get it right,' said a voice behind them, that was easily recognised. Leda Hintzen, of course . . . well, who else? Anne turned round to face her, and to face Charles, who was standing by her side. 'I dragged Charles here to see my efforts,' Leda said to Susan Cleaver.

'You painted all this?' Susan touched the scenery.

'She did,' said Charles, 'and the mansion at the other end,' he looked towards Toad Hall.

Leda enquired about Susan's baby, and the two began to chat. Charles, his head avoiding a hanging cut-out of Mickey Mouse, asked Anne how she was. 'I heard Mrs Pentrose went home,' he remarked.

'Yes, yesterday, and I'm well, thank you.' Her mouth felt very dry, and her face tight, but she managed to get it to move. She hadn't seen Charles to speak to for days—not for seventeen days, not since the day they had met at her grandmother's bed. He had been into Livingstone for the ward rounds, as had the Professor, but the day-to-day work was done by Susan now.

'It's very quiet in here, for once,' he remarked conversationally. 'Most of the children are sent home for Christmas, those that can be moved. These little ones,' his eye did a scan of the occupied beds and cots, 'have their mothers in to look after them for part of every day.' He went over to speak to a three-year-old girl, with a heavily bandaged head. Both her arms had been loosely splinted with corrugated paper, to stop her bending them up and trying to drag her dressings off.

'I'm a Dalek,' she said, moving her straightened arms up and down like a robot. She looked a forlorn but spunky little scrap.

'Road accident case . . . lost her right eye . . . both her parents were killed,' Sister informed them, as they made their way out of the ward. Susan Cleaver and Leda were some way behind, but Anne felt she ought to get back. She said so to Charles, and made to leave him, but he fell into step beside her.

'How are the dogs?' he asked.

'Oh, fine,' she said, 'and Queenie's had her litter . . . two girls and a boy, born last Monday, at intervals during the day. So Mrs Thirle was the one in charge—I think Ray felt quite cheated! She, Mrs Thirle, called Will Grainger in, just in case of trouble, but there wasn't any; everything went off well.'

'Is Gilbertson still with you?'

'Not at the Cottage, no. Nella's got her sister with her, till I have my two weeks' leave. After that she should be able to manage on her own.'

'How much longer have you got on Livingstone?' He watched her button her cape and fold it to her, as they reached the outside doors.

'Just on three weeks, then it's back to Block to consolidate all I've learned, then home for a fortnight, then Block again to prepare for another ward, which I'm told is likely to be Women's Surgical.'

'Will you be sorry?'

'To leave Livingstone, you mean?'

He nodded, and she shook her head. 'No, I won't. I like change, I'm anxious to move on.' The words came out, and she seemed to see them floating in the air, and she couldn't believe she had actually said them, said them with such deliberateness . . . and cut and thrust . . . and sheer untruthfulness. Why had she said them, *why*, and what on earth was she trying to do? I'm trying not to mind that he's bound up with Leda Hintzen; I'm trying to convince myself that he doesn't matter to me; I'm trying my hardest to armour myself against the onslaughts he makes on my heart and mind and body and inner peace. I don't want . . . I will not have . . . I *won't* be disturbed like that! He shan't do it . . . I *will* not give him the chance!

'Oh well, as you're so enamoured of change,' he said in equable tones, 'you'll not be averse to a sea of new faces . . . you'll cut adrift easily.'

'I've had to learn to do so, haven't I?' And now she sounded self-pitying. He'd think she was touting for sympathy, which she wasn't, and oh, why *was* it that he always made her show the worst side of herself?

The other two caught up with them. They began to cross the yard. The fir tree invoked comment again, and Susan Cleaver asked Leda where she was spending the Christmas holiday.

'Here in London. I've got a new flat out at Martle Rise—the one at Camden was far too small. You thought so, didn't you, Charles?'

'I did.' He thrust his hands in his pockets, his chin into the air.

'It was claustrophobic, and I'm certain it caused many of my headaches. It's so easy to get here from Martle Rise, either by car or tube. It's just temporary, of course, until . . .' Leda's words were drowned by a passing ambulance. Within its discordant up-and-down sound Anne excused herself, thanking Susan for taking her over to Paeds.

'Only too glad.' Susan watched her go, making for Beyton Wing, cape flying out, head bent against the wind. 'Now that,' she said, looking at Charles, 'is a very nice girl indeed. She'll make a first-class nurse one day, unless she decides to get married and throw it all up before she's fully trained.'

'She's going out with a one-time patient,' Leda told her, 'an Australian, so they somewhat naturally gravitated together. He's over here for three years, which is rather significant, because by that time she'll have qualified; she's bright enough, I'm sure. And an SRN can get a job anywhere in the world, especially the ones that are London-trained.'

'Oh, I see.' Susan looked back at her, and at Charles for confirmation. He was scraping a piece of paper off his shoe.

'She's bound to go back with him,' Leda went on, 'you can tell they are very attached. And she hates England, she told me so,' she added for good measure . . . a pale lie wouldn't blacken her soul. She, too, looked at Charles, who muttered about the time, and sped off to Women's Medical.

Anne was nearly ten minutes late back on Livingstone. 'I thought you were never coming,' grumbled Ellen. 'Where on earth have you been?' Without waiting to hear her reply, she hurried off to her own break. Repinning her cap, and collecting her thoughts, and dismissing Charles from her mind, Anne went to deal with Mr Cadman, the deaf man with emphysema, who had spilled his malted milk over his blanket and sheet.

By breakfast-time on Christmas Eve there were three vacant beds in Livingstone, and each of the two side wards was vacant too. Sister Grant, the day before, had agreed that one of the latter could be used as a little Christmas den for the staff. They were able to put their cards in there, trim it up as they pleased, put goodies and presents, many of them given by generous patients, on a trestle table covered with a sheet. Trails of ivy drooped from the sills, tinsel outlined the windows, mistletoe hung from a string above the door.

The work routine went on the same, nothing was overlooked, but the atmosphere of suppressed excitement that abounded amongst the staff seemed to penetrate every crack and crevice and ceiling and floor. 'It's the Christmas fever,' Tessa Merrow said, 'and it's nothing to do temperatures!' She and Anne were tidying lockers before the round.

Charles did the round, he was on his own, he had six patients to see, but he went to each bed afterwards, and into the day room too, to wish everyone a happy time in spite of their various ills. Mr Jarman, the rheumatoid arthritic, by his bed in a wheelchair, demonstrated how improved he was by pinning a sprig of holly—with immense difficulty and great concentration—on to the front of Charles' coat. 'There you are, Doc! Just for you!' He sat back, sucking his thumb, well pricked by holly and safety-pin combined.

'That's the best present I've had yet,' Anne heard Charles reply, just before Sister whisked him out and took him into her room.

'She's giving him a nip of sherry . . . it's the norm for Christmas Eve!' Jane Lyne whispered; she could see them through the glass.

Anne was in the side ward, setting some cards on the table, when Sister brought Charles in . . . he didn't look over-pleased. It might have been Anne's imagination, but his face seemed to tighten up when he saw her there. Sister went gaily on: 'Now, don't you think my nurses have made a wonderful job of this room? You'd not recognise it, would you?' Her smile included Anne. 'And this is your first experience of Christmas in hospital, isn't it, Nurse?'

'Yes, it is, and I'm glad to be here,' she said simply and truthfully. To have been in Melbourne without her parents, especially at this time of year, would have brought back many crowding memories, would have forced comparisons, would have made it a time of sadness instead of joy. There was sadness here too, one couldn't avoid it, but being extra busy, and having to work with others as a team, had a steadying influence, even if one couldn't have everything one wanted; she met Charles' eyes and hastily looked at the floor.

Sister, not knowing about her parents, merely thought her reply polite. She was just about to remind her to go to her coffee break, when the Reverend Mr Folkham, the hospital chaplain, put his bald head round the door. 'Oh, Mr Folkham, I need to see you about the midnight service!' Out she went, slamming the door and disturbing the bunch of mistletoe, which fell in a heap practically on Charles' feet. He picked it up, re-tied it, hung it more securely and gave it a little pushing, testing swing.

'Mistletoe isn't the easiest of greenery to arrange artistically. It's a parasite, likes something to cling to.' He brought his hand down too sharply and inadvertently knocked Anne's cap askew. 'I'm so sorry!' He made to straighten it, then stepped back and left it to her.

'I can do it, thank you.' She moved away, and refixed it at the mirror. Her reflection stared back at her, framed in tinsel; she could see him standing behind her, making a 'backdrop', like Leda's scenery.

'I'd like to wish you a happy Christmas,' she could see his lips forming the words, even more plainly than she could hear them; she turned and smiled her thanks.

'I wish you one too.' Her gaze locked with his, but no closeness eased the moment, each guarded their own feelings, and the light touch of his hands—one on each side of her stiff white collar—meant nothing much at all. It was no more than he would give a patient, but what did she expect? She thought of the two of them at the Cottage, of the sunlight on the snow, of Charles in the orchard, of Charles in the kitchen, of the two of them having breakfast . . . of sliding down the garden path, and having him catch her, and hold her . . . but all that had just been an interlude. It was fairly obvious that he and Leda were having an affair . . . an affair, moreover,

that might lead to marriage . . . Leda had hinted at that
. . . 'we both love children, *fortunately*'. Anne had never
forgotten those words, nor what they portended; she
thought of them now, and moved back to the door.

'I'd better go, or I'll miss my break.' Her fingers felt
for the handle. 'All the very best, Doctor. I hope you
have a good time.'

The mistletoe fell down yet again as she hurried up the
passage. This time it stayed where it was on the floor,
and he didn't even see it, nor feel it under his feet as he
left the room.

It was Padre Folkham who organised the evening
carol singing. Student nurses from various wards, total-
ing forty in all, assembled in the Nurses' Home, wearing
their cloaks inside out—with the brilliant scarlet lining
showing, holly trims on their caps. They each carried a
lantern at the end of a pole, similar to the kind carried
aloft by singers in Dickens' days. Anne and Pru were
amongst them, as were most of their fellow students
whom they would see again when they all returned to
Block. Pru was excited and happy and flushed, her
round face taking the glow of the lantern she carried,
and the colour of her cloak; Pru was ashine, and aglow
with love. Tom was the lucky man.

The little crocodile crossed the yard, shepherded by
the padre, and accompanied by a clerk from Admin who
trundled a portable organ. They were to visit only those
wards which had been especially selected, thus avoiding
any chance of possible disturbance to patients who might
be too ill to listen to them.

It was great fun; it was also moving and, to Anne, a
new experience. They grouped themselves in the softly-
lit wards, holding up their lanterns, singing all the best
loved carols, and being joined at times by one or two of
the patients who were well enough to be up. There was a

senior nurse in every corridor to hush and shush the singers when excitement proved too much for them, as they moved from ward to ward. When it was over they all piled into the nurses' dining-room for mince pies and coffee, and greetings and laughter and chat.

Next came the Midnight Service, and the hospital chapel was packed. Doctors and surgeons stood at the back, others crowded the porch. The pulpit was banked with chrysanthemums, and their sharp nostalgic scent reached Anne as she sat near the front, squashed between Ellen and Pru. Emotion was very hard to contain, yet the atmosphere was peace. It was goodwill too, and the ancient walls that had stood for centuries breathed it out, and echoed the padre's words. Even the stained-glass windows moved, and brought their portrayals to life in the light of the candles flickering in the draught.

The highlight of Christmas Day was lunch which, because of the various diets, was to some extent dimmed on Livingstone Ward. Even so, it was much enjoyed, and the kitchens did mammoth work, sending down traditional fare—so far as was allowed—on piping hot plates, all ready for handing out. The staff had theirs in the dining-room, for gone were the days when senior consultants appeared on each ward to carve a gargantuan turkey and sit down with the nurses to eat it there.

After lunch there were visits to other wards, to exchange more greetings. Anne paid a flying visit to Pru. Geriatrics was as gay as the children's ward, and most of the elderlies were up and about, or through in the day room, watching television, or entertaining visitors by their beds.

Pru and Tom were both on duty, and it was there in one of the side wards, also used as a Christmas room, like the one on Livingstone, that they told her they were engaged to be married. 'Tom asked me this morning,

Anne,' Pru held out her left hand, proudly displaying her ring. It was a diamond cluster, it winked in the light, and Pru's thumb rubbed it lovingly. 'On an ordinary day I wouldn't be able to wear it on the ward, but as it's Christmas . . .'

'Oh, Pru, how *lovely*!' Anne gave her an outsize hug. 'I'm so pleased . . . I'm very pleased! Congratulations, Tom!'

'It all seems very fitting to me,' Tom said prosaically. And he was, thought Anne, shaking his hand, exactly right for Pru. She was very young, but steady too; she was warmhearted and caring; she could cook too, and Tom so liked his food.

'Tom's got a flat at Martle Rise,' Pru prattled on. 'He was going to buy it, anyway . . . he doesn't like living-in. Miss Hintzen put him on to it—she knows the area. A friend of hers has bought a house there, and Miss Hintzen rents the top. The flat Tom's buying is in a new block—a purpose-built block of flats. I saw it last week, but he hadn't actually asked me to marry him then. Actually, Anne, I thought,' she added, when Tom had excused himself, 'that he was going to ask me to live there with him, and I expect I would have done, but I'd rather be married. I'd like to be settled for good.'

'I'm sure you'll be very happy, I'm pleased,' Anne said again. 'We'll celebrate tonight, shall we? Ray's coming up from Dowford. I must go now, Rose Logan's on duty, and I'll have to start the teas.' She caught sight of Dr Cleaver passing the side ward door. She ran to catch up with her; Susan's colour was high.

'I've been having a glass of port with old Mrs Robinson,' she explained. 'She's ninety-five and she takes her liquor a sight better than me. I'm off to Livingstone now, Anne; you can give me a glass of bicarb. Somehow or other I've got to keep fit and awake for the rest of the day. I could just imagine what Charles would say if I fell asleep on the job!'

'He's not inhuman.'

'Very far from it,' Susan's glance held amusement. 'He's got a lovely sense of humour too, which I dare say he needs, with the lady from Holland dogging his every move.'

'But I thought . . .' Anne began.

'You thought what?' They were climbing the stairs, all the lifts were taken.

'I thought it was a two-way thing.'

'To a certain extent it may be. I mean, look at her, she's attractive, and Charles, as you've just said yourself, is human, and male to boot, and *I'm* talking too much. I ought to be more circumspect,' said Susan a few minutes later, drinking a glass of mist.mag.trisil in the privacy of the kitchen, back on the ward, and looking over at Anne. 'Doctors shouldn't gossip, but I'll stick my neck out and say that I think she does most of the chasing, and if he lets it go on, and if he allows himself to be caught—and I mean in matrimony—then it's either his own deep-seated wish, or she's got some hold on him.'

Anne found herself devoid of words; she just stared at Susan's back, as she stood at the sink, rinsing out her glass. 'I'm on his side,' Susan turned round, running a hand through her curls, 'nevertheless, my opinion is that at some time or other—and remember he knew her long before she appeared at the Walbrook—my opinion is that something happened that still binds him up with her. I could be wrong, but that's what I think. Sometimes she throws out hints. And now, having let drop those pearls of wisdom,' she buttoned up her coat, 'I'll go in and see how our Mr Cadman's standing up to the strain of four visitors, instead of his customary two.'

As it was Christmas Day, visitors were given tea as well. Left alone in the kitchen, Anne began to assemble the cups. Not for one moment did she take seriously what Susan Cleaver had said. Charles Farne wasn't the kind of man to have a shady past. He wasn't the kind to allow any woman, or any*one*, for that matter, to put pressure on him, or try to force his hand.

CHAPTER NINE

'THERE'S no reason why you and I shouldn't take a flat together,' said Ray the evening before he went up to Scotland to spend the New Year with cousins in Edinburgh. 'And I don't mean shack-up in the fullest sense,' he caught the look on Anne's face, 'but we could rent a sizeable furnished flat, share it as friends, if you liked. It would be great, Anne . . . I'd love it. We could get to know one another, instead of meeting in fits and starts, and having nowhere to go. If we found a place roughly midway between Dowford and the hospital, it would be okay for both of us, a nine-mile journey's nothing. You'll miss Pru when she gets married, and you can't *like* living-in, any more than I like living en famille with the Lowes. We could share expenses, and everything. I think we'd get on fine. You might even get to like me better.' He paused to get his breath. Anne found hers, and tried her best to choose refusing words that wouldn't sound as though she were slapping him down without proper thought.

'I like you *now*, Ray,' she smiled at him, 'but I don't want to move at the moment. Cade House is very comfortable, and I don't like travelling. I feel that while I'm training I want to be on the spot.'

'Tactfully put!' He didn't argue, he even smiled back at her, but his colour changed, and his gaze was a little fixed.

'But I think,' she went on quickly, 'that a flat might be fine for you. You're here for three years, and that's a long time to feel dissatisfied.' Heavens, she thought, I'm

139

putting this badly. She pushed her plate on one side; they were having supper at a small trattoria near to the hospital. It was Ray's birthday too, which made it even worse. 'I think, if you really want a flat, you should try for one,' she told him. 'Without me to consider, you could get one nearer to Dowford, even perhaps *in* Dowford, where the rent wouldn't be so high.'

'I don't think I'll bother.' His bottom lip jutted.

'I'm very sorry, Ray,' she sighed.

'No matter . . . let's leave it.' He began to tell her about his Scottish cousins, whom he had never met, but who had promised him a traditional Hogmanay. The cloud of embarrassment took itself off; Anne told him about her own plans, yet somehow or other (and she felt this strongly) things weren't the same between them. She had hurt his pride, and upset his ideas; he had set his sights on a flat—a place to which they could both have come back every single night, and made it home; he had thought she would feel the same. She didn't, and couldn't, and she had had to tell him, so of course he wasn't pleased. I'm so sorry, Ray, she thought miserably . . . I really am so sorry. I just wish you hadn't brought the subject up.

As things turned out, her own plans for New Year's Eve were quashed. The 'flu epidemic amongst the staff, which had started just after Christmas, meant that the duty rosters had to be changed. A fifth of the staff were off sick, and the nursing officers were at their wits' end to know how to cover the wards. Livingstone Ward had an agency nurse to do the work of Rose Logan and Ellen, who were both stricken at the same time. As for Anne, she was summoned to Sister's office after breakfast on New Year's Eve. She was surprised, and a little apprehensive, to see Sister Tutor there, stately as ever, bust sticking out like a prow.

'We've just been talking about you, Nurse.' Sister Grant's welcoming smile banished the further foreboding Anne had felt at her words. Sister Tutor merely nodded, and trumpeted into her hanky.

'It's only a cold, I don't have 'flu,' she said with a further sniff. 'Yes, Sister, please go on.' Sister did, and came to the point.

'Can you, Anne, at very short notice, rearrange your plans, and do the night shift here on Livingstone . . . *tonight*, I mean, New Year's Eve? I expect you were going home, were you not?'

'Yes, Sister, this afternoon.'

'Can you put it off? Can you do the shift? I think you're up to it. Your reports so far (this was Sister Tutor) have been fairly satisfactory. There would be an SRN with you, of course, you wouldn't be on your own.'

Sister Grant broke in at that point, smiling at Anne from her desk. 'It's very short notice, we know that, so we're not insisting you do it. If you can't then we'll contact the agency, but both Sister Tutor and I feel it would be a very useful adjunct to your training. In the ordinary way night duty experience doesn't come until later on.'

So they're almost, Anne thought, with a flicker of amusement, doing me a favour. But it *is* only for the one night, and I'm not doing anything special, and Nella will be the first to understand. She agreed, therefore, to do as they asked, and was sent off duty at once. 'Go back to the Nurses' Home and rest, even if you can't sleep. Report back here at eight p.m., then after breakfast tomorrow you'll be free until Wednesday midday.' Sister was altering the roster. 'Jane Lyne and Ellen will be back on Monday, when we won't have so many problems.'

Feeling a little as though she were skiving, Anne

returned to the Nurses' Home. Changing out of her
uniform into skirt and sweater and boots, she settled
down by the radiator and wrote to Grandfather Martin,
her late mother's father, out in Canberra. She wrote two
more letters to friends in Melbourne, then debated what
to do next. It was unthinkable to go to bed yet, she
hadn't long been up. On the other hand, she stared out
of the window, the day was hardly inviting. There wasn't
a ray of sun to be seen, it was scarcely even light; the
wind was a strong north-easterly, gusting, the weather-
man said, to hurricane force down on the Sussex coast.
But that's not here, and I'm not made of glass, thought
Anne; I'll walk down to Bank, and get the Tube to
Oxford Circus, and join the scrum at the sales. I need
some clothes, warm ones, and at the same time,
perhaps, I can look around for a wedding gift for
Pru.

To get to the nearest exit gate, she had to pass
Pendleton Wing, then the ugly but functional building
which was the Doctors' Residence. There was a post-box
set in the wall, she would put her letters in there.
Stopping to pull them out of her bag, she didn't see
Charles Farne part company with a junior colleague,
then cross the path to her. 'Good morning, Nurse . . .
just off for New Year?'

The sound of his voice made her jump, and she looked
up, sliding the zip on her bag, her other hand clutching
the letters. 'Good morning, Doctor—no, I'm not going
home, not till tomorrow morning.' One of her letters
dropped to the ground, and he stooped and picked it up;
as he straightened he looked at the others still in her
hand.

'Like me to put them in for you?' he jerked his head at
the box.

'Thank you, that's kind.'

His shoulders were squared, his back view long and dark. He wasn't wearing his white coat, so perhaps he wasn't on duty, which might account for his casual friendliness. With the donning of his white coat, he retreated as if behind walls, Anne thought, wondering if she should wait.

Charles released the letters and heard them drop with a rustle into the box. He had noticed, he could hardly fail to, the striped-bordered envelopes. Airmail letters . . . perhaps to Australia . . . letters across the miles, letters to a land that was drenched with sun . . . a sun to warm one's bones. January in England, the killer month. He thought of his father and sickened, then turned round to Anne with a face so white that she stared at him in alarm.

'You look . . . frozen!' She took a step forward, then felt him grasp her arm.

'I *am* frozen . . . to the marrow, as they say.' She was relieved to see him smile. 'Come and have a coffee with me. Can you bear the Hospital shop? It doesn't look all that crowded at the moment,' they could see it from where they stood, 'and their coffee brew beats the vending machine, convenient though it is.'

'Thank you, I'd love one. I'm going to the sales, so I need some sustenance.' They began to walk over to the Hospital shop, which was also a coffee bar. It was mainly for the outdoor and ancillary staff, but all grades could use it. It got crowded in rushes, as shifts and duties changed.

'You're doing something wildly exciting in Town tonight, I suppose?' remarked Charles, as they perched on stools and stirred dark brown sugar into tall beakers of coffee topped with cream.

'Not really, no. I'm working. I'm doing the night shift,' she told him, 'on Livingstone. Sister's just asked me . . . it's because of the 'flu epidemic.'

'Oh dear, that's tough,' his eyebrows went up. 'New Year's Eve is special.'

'Yes . . . well, it can't be helped.' The coffee ran warm down her throat. 'I can go home early tomorrow. I rang Nella and explained, and she said Great-Aunt Flo—that's her sister—would drive up and fetch me; otherwise travelling might be tricky, it being New Year's Day.'

'Can't Gilbertson fetch you?' asked Charles.

'Ray is in Scotland.'

'A good place to spend the New Year.'

'He's got relatives there,' she explained.

'Oh yes, I see.'

Their talk slowed down to a halt. Somehow or other it always did whenever Ray was mentioned. To try to get it going again, Anne asked if he'd had a good Christmas. Instantly she wished she hadn't, for the strained look came back to his face. It was her fault, she'd caused it, she'd blundered, but how . . . what could be wrong? Had he quarrelled with Leda, because that would do it . . . had something happened between them? She had gone to Holland for the New Year, Anne had heard her telling Sister that she was flying to Amsterdam on the twenty-eighth of December, so perhaps . . .

'Our Christmas was very mixed,' said Charles, pushing his cup on one side. He glanced at Anne, seemed about to say more, then abruptly changed his mind as a crowd of workers from Sterile Supply came charging through the doors and up to the counter, squeezing between the stools. 'We'd better shift ourselves, don't you think . . . if you've finished, that is?' He leaned backwards to shout this to Anne across the width of a large young man who was queueing up for a coffee and a ham roll.

'I agree, yes . . . and I've finished, thanks.' With such

a din in her ears, she was glad enough to get outside, but she hoped, nevertheless, that Charles might walk with her to the gates. He didn't, he made no move to. He took his leave of her right outside the glass doors of the shop which had steamed up in the rush.

'They could do with enlarging that place to more than twice its size,' he remarked. He said nothing else about his 'mixed Christmas', so of course she couldn't ask.

'Thank you for the coffee,' she said, and all he did was nod, and mutter about Dr Susan Cleaver, and seeing that she got off duty to spend the weekend with her husband and family.

'Good luck with your shopping,' he added, 'and don't spend all your hard-earned cash.'

And with that they turned and separated, each on their different ploys—Charles to Casualty, where he'd last seen Susan, she to the exit gates, and Bank Underground, and Selfridges, and the sales. We just meet and part, and nothing happens, Anne thought with flash of anger. But why am I angry, and what on earth do I mean, *or* expect? Put him out of your mind . . . forget him. But she found that hard to do. The shadow or shade of Charles Farne walked beside her all morning. Try as she might, she couldn't get rid of the man.

There were two new patients in Livingstone Ward when Nurse Alicia James and a rather apprehensive Anne went on duty that night. One was a hypothermia case—a man of sixty-eight. He had been brought in covered in tinfoil to conserve what heat he had. He was in the first of the side wards, swaddled in warm blankets, and extra heating had been turned on in the room. It appeared he had been unwell for some weeks, there were signs of dehydration. To correct this he was being infused with a warmed solution of dextrose. His pulse was slow, his breathing was shallow, and he was on

quarter-hourly obs. 'You can manage those, I hope?'
Nurse James enquired of Anne. 'I take it you also know
how to change his infusion bottle?'

'Yes, Staff,' Anne nodded assent, and was swept into
the ward to see Mr Gilpin, the other new patient, who
was suffering from renal colic. He was wide awake, and
sweating profusely; at a gesture from Nurse James,
Anne wiped his forehead with a moist cold flannel
lying in a dish on his locker. Nurse James walked
away, beckoning Anne to the desk; she was reading
Mr Gilpin's notes.

'He had his last Peth injection four hours ago,' she
said, 'looks like he's going to need another. In the
meantime fill his hot bottle, make sure it's properly
covered and put it against his loin. Do what you can to
reassure him, sit with him for a bit. *I'll* do the first of the
observations on Mr Carnie. If Gilpin should start to
vomit again, ring the bell at once. You know all the other
patients, don't you . . . better than me, I dare say!' And
with that she was off, a tall, pale girl, with long spindly
legs. In the dimmed light of the ward she looked like an
airy flitting moth, her feet scarcely touching the polished
floor.

Anne exchanged Mr Gilpin's cool bottle with a hot
one, then helped him turn on to his side. He asked her if
he was going to die, and she assured him that he was not.

'Feels like it . . . don't care if I do,' he muttered.

'You'll feel better presently. We'll give you another
injection in a minute, then the pain will ease away. I'll
stay here with you till Staff comes back.' Once more she
wiped his forehead, then sat with him till Alicia James
returned.

At eleven o'clock the Night Superintendent came to
do her round, and soon after that Nurse James asked the
kitchens to send down two supper trays. 'They're for us,'

she said, 'you can have yours first . . . use Sister's office. We'll give the dining-room a miss tonight, it'll save us precious time, and as you're new I don't suppose you want to be left on your own.'

Agreeing that that was the last thing she wanted, Anne went along to the side ward to do the next set of observations on the hypothermia case. They were satisfactory, very much so . . . his temperature was up, so was his blood pressure, and his breathing was stronger; he was going to be all right. He was falling asleep almost before Anne had finished tucking him up. You were lucky your neighbour found you in time, she told the slumbering man. You'll be here a week or two, I dare say, then when you leave us for good we'll contact the Social Services to make sure you're supervised. And he probably wouldn't like that at all, but what was the alternative? Everyone needed a helping hand at times.

By eleven-thirty both nurses had eaten—without a good deal of relish—the turkey rissoles and cold mince tart sent down by the night kitchen staff. Nurse James repaired to the ward desk, suggesting Anne made some tea: 'But bring it in quietly, for goodness' sake, or half the ward will want it!' Anne did as she said, and was creeping back to the kitchen to have her own when she stopped stunt in the nick of time, just managing to avoid the white-sheathed figure of Charles Farne standing outside the doors:

'Goodness, you startled me!' she laughed confusedly, waiting for him to pass. 'Do you want Staff? Has she bleeped you?'

'No, nothing like that.' He looked through the doors, but didn't go in. He turned round to Anne again. 'I was next door in Women's Med, so thought I'd give you a look, mainly to check on the new admissions.'

'Staff Nurse is in the ward,' she told him.

'I see she is, but can't *you* brief me?' He took off his stethoscope, as though he felt, or at any rate hoped, he had finished for the night.

'Mr Carnie's coming to nicely. I've just done his last set of obs.' She gave him the details, and he nodded, looking pleased.

'Best let him sleep now,' he said, 'don't disturb him unless you're alarmed. What about Mr Gilpin?' Again she gave him concise details. He listened, his eyes on her face. 'I'll see him tomorrow morning, before the shift changes over.' Then he looked towards the kitchen door. 'Would that be tea I can smell?'

'It would. I've just made some.'

'Any chance of a cup? I've been down in Casualty. It's all systems go down there tonight, it being a Saturday *and* New Year's Eve . . . the peak time for accidents.'

Anne led the way into the kitchen. 'Of course you can have some,' she said. 'Would you like me to bring it to Sister's Office?' She slipped another tea-bag into the pot and boiled up the kettle again.

'No, thanks, I'll have it in here with you.' Charles pulled a chair up to the table. She took the pot to the sink to pour out; she couldn't trust her hand to deliver a straight stream of scalding hot tea into each of the cups—not with him watching her, not with him sitting so close. 'So, how's the night shift going?' he asked, when she joined him at the table, passing his tea, which he drank in grateful sips.

'Not too bad. I think all right.' She met his eyes and smiled. 'It feels entirely different, though . . . the whole place does, at night. Everything changes, even the patients, the atmosphere, the lot . . . even *I* feel different!' She put down her cup with a bump.

'In what way?'

She felt that his eyes saw every thought in her head.

She tried to explain what she meant. 'Well, for one thing, without the daytime noises I'm almost afraid to move. I feel I ought to tiptoe about and whisper, and not clatter things. In trying so hard to be quiet I get clumsier by the hour!'

'You're doing all right, and I doubt if you're clumsy, I doubt that very much. I can't imagine you other than graceful, and very, very deft.' His gaze dropped to her long slender fingers curled round the bowl of her cup. There was an ink mark on the bib of her apron, another blue mark on her chin. Her chin moved, as she smiled and started to speak.

'What a nice thing to say!' A pink tide of embarrassment and pleasure flowed into her face, and out again. She all but dropped her cup. The compliment and the look Charles gave her made her heart turn over. Even at the Cottage he'd not been like this, so perhaps he was different too. Perhaps the hospital night wrought a change in everyone. Then, as if to confound her, he made a gesture so annoying and familiar that she wanted to strike him . . . he moved and looked at his watch. 'If you want to go, do so,' she said, and now anger made her flush. 'I expect you're tired, you'll want to catch up on your sleep!'

'Not so.' He sounded amused, yet anxious too, perhaps. 'It's five minutes to midnight, Anne—there are five minutes left of the year. I want to see the New Year in with you. Is that so . . . reprehensible?'

'No!' the word shot out of her, then: 'No, of course it's not,' she said more quietly, watching him as he opened the window a crack.

'To hear the first of the bells,' he said, 'not that they *all* ring, mind. Come . . .' he held out his hand to her, and she went and stood at his side, feeling the chill from the open window, feeling the warmth of his arm hugging her shoulders. This couldn't be happening . . .. was it really happening? They stood at the window, waiting for the bells. When they came they seemed to carol in relays. 'It's a trick of the ears, and the wind, and distance too,' Charles explained, 'because of course they all start at once.' He turned her so that she faced him. 'A happy New Year to you, Anne.'

'And to you.'

He bent and kissed her, a salutary kind of kiss, the kind of kiss people tend to exchange on such a special Eve. But then, as she made to move away, he caught her and jerked her close. Startled, she said his name just once before his mouth sought hers, before she soared away with him into a new dimension, where nothing existed except emotion, where thinking had no place, where feeling prevailed, and nothing, nothing else.

As his arms loosened the world sifted back—the chill from the window at first, then the bells again, cascading and pealing, then a more insistent sound, nearer at hand, which she strove to identify.

'It's the phone in Sister's office,' his words came into her ear. He held her within the circle of his arm, his other hand stroked her hair.

'I must answer it.' She stepped backwards, forcing her legs to move.

'It's being answered already,' the buzzing sound had ceased, 'and for God's sake look at me!' The sight of her back enraged him; it enslaved him too, but he wouldn't admit that, not for a single second. 'There's no need to behave as though we've committed some kind of heinous sin!'

'Of course not.' Anne turned round, arms upraised to her cap, her hands making futile pushing movements in the thicknesses of her hair. Where was her cap? She picked it up, just as the door was opened, just as a voice said:

'Oh, you *are* here, Doctor.' And the mothlike figure of Staff Nurse James stood in the aperture. 'You're wanted on the phone,' she said, 'it's an outside call . . . long distance.'

'Many thanks,' snapped Charles, and his going was swift. Nurse James looked at Anne.

'You should have told me he was here, you know.'

'I'm sorry.' Anne looked at her feet.

'And if there's any tea left in that pot, I could do with another cup.'

'I'm sure there is.' Anne poured it out, while Alicia James perched on the table. She was plainly determined to be in evidence when Charles Farne reappeared. When he came neither she nor Anne heard him till he was standing in the doorway. He was holding on to either jamb as though he were nailed to a cross.

'I've had bad news—my father has died, I have to go home at once.' A shocked expletive came from Nurse James, while Anne could only stare. 'You'll have to get on to Dr Cleaver,' his voice was clipped and terse, 'she'll have to take over, have to fill in. Oh, and ring the Professor too . . . in the morning for him, of course, it's too late tonight.'

'Yes, Doctor, I'll do it at once—ring Dr Cleaver, I mean.' Alicia James walked towards him and he moved to let her pass. 'I'm so sorry, I really am, Dr Farne . . . if there's anything else I can do?'

'Nothing at all, Staff, thanks just the same.' He watched her go to the office; then he turned with a clumsy, fumbling movement into the corridor.

'Please wait!' The words burst from Anne. 'Can't I do *something* to help?'

At first it seemed he wouldn't heed her, wouldn't even

stop. He was walking swiftly towards the doors; she ran to keep up with him. Then he stopped and gripped her hand tightly in his. 'Just be here when I get back.'

'Of course I will.'

He punched through the doors, crossed the landing and descended the stairs. Anne stood and listened to the sound of his footfalls. Oh, if only she could go with him! If only she could . . . if only . . . if only . . . if only she didn't love him . . .

But she knew she did, and she knew she always would.

CHAPTER TEN

CHARLES was still at Seftonbridge the following Monday week, when Leda came into the ward to help a much-improved Mr Carnie weave a basketwork edge to a fancy tray.

When Jane Lyne, rather tentatively, mentioned the death of Charles' father, Leda thanked her and agreed it was very sad. 'He had been ill for over a year, though, they knew it was terminal. Charles thought he might see another spring, so did Mrs Farne. She's a GP, as her husband was, so they both knew the score. It has been a dreadful time all round, and blocked so many plans.'

Anne could hear the conversation as she sat at the ward desk. She couldn't help wondering which was worse—to lose a parent suddenly, or to have him desperately ill for a year, knowing he couldn't get well. She felt a gnaw of compassion for Charles, along with a deepseated jealousy of Leda, who was in his confidence. He'll turn to her, not to me, I'll have to prepare for that, she thought. But he has said . . . *he had said* . . .' be here when I get back'. Yet that could have been a tripped-out phrase, said on the spur of the moment. I'm reading too much into everything, she thought, indulging in wishful thinking, and hopeless dreams, and I can't seem to stop myself. Did Leda know when Charles would be back? She and Staff Nurse were still talking, but what they were saying became inaudible, as Mrs Floss, the librarian, was passing by, calling out to Anne:

'I've just left Mr Gilpin with one of those horse-racing novels. I thought it might take his mind off his trouble

. . . awful things, those stones. My husband got rid of his by drinking pints of barley water. He's never had a speck of trouble since.'

'I'm glad to hear it,' said Anne, watching Leda Hintzen get up and make her way to the doors. Dr Cleaver was coming in, and the two women stopped to chat. Jane Lyne brought some charts to the desk and reminded Anne of the time: 'It's three-thirty, Nurse.' Anne went to start the teas.

Two days later, on the day before Charles was due to return, Ellen Tillot, who had been down to Casualty to borrow some paper sheets, buttonholed Anne in the linen room. 'You'll never guess what!' She was breathless from running, as she pushed Anne farther in and shut the door, leaning against the shelves. 'A baby's come in, been brought in to Casualty, a little boy of two. I was at the reception counter when this woman, a Mrs Johns, came in with him grizzling in her arms. She'd come in from Martle Rise, she said . . . he'd caught his hand in a door. She was a foreign woman, German or Dutch; she said Miss Hintzen must come. The kid was yelling by this time, and Meg Hall, the receptionist, wanted to fill in the usual forms, but the woman said Hintzen must come. She said Leda Hintzen was the child's mother . . . his *mother*, Anne, do you hear! She said Leda rented the top of her house, and she and the child lived there. She, the woman, looked after him while Leda was at work, but he'd hurt his hand and she thought it was broken, so she brought him straight here. He'd only been in England a week, she said, Leda brought him from Amsterdam after the New Year holiday, and now this had to happen . . . you should have heard her! She just went on and on.'

'And you stopped and listened?' Anne's head was bursting; the little room was airless. She pushed past and opened the door, but couldn't quite bring herself to walk away and not hear the rest of the tale. She was quite sure there was more to come, there was something about Ellen's face that told her that . ... it was avid and excited, she could hardly get her words out.

'Well, anyway, they sent for Hintzen, and you should have seen her, Anne! She grabbed that kid and sat down with him, rocking him in her arms. She looked all soft and maternal, it was hard to believe it was her. I was still at the counter, she didn't even see me—well, I *did* draw back a bit. They went through to the cubicles, Leda carrying the boy. He'd stopped yelling then, she'd taken his hood off and unzipped his coat. He was redheaded, Anne . . . he had curly hair in that gorgeous copper-beech shade. And what did I deduce from that . . . what would *anyone* deduce? If he's not Charles Farne's son, then I'm Florence Nightingale! How about that for a rousing item of news!'

Ellen's face seemed to dwindle, then loom again, her eyes were as big as a cat's, then small and pinpointed. Anne found her voice at last. 'Rousing news or not, Ellen, I should keep it to yourself. You could easily be wrong; two-year-olds have no features to speak of; they're just—well, babies, with faces like blobs.'

'They have hair, though—hair and eyes—you don't see that colour hair often. And as Hintzen and Farne keep close company, and have done for some years . . .'

'All the same—' Anne felt angry, confused, furious with Ellen. She wasn't even sure she believed her; the child might be Leda's baby, but the rest Ellen had made up. I don't believe the rest, I just don't believe it, she thought to herself, then said with a touch of frost: 'I should watch what you're saying, Ellen. Talk like that causes trouble. Now, if you don't mind, I'd like to get on with checking the rest of this linen. Those disposable sheets,' she looked at the rolls under Ellen's arm, 'are wanted in clean utility, Nurse Logan's been asking for them.' The word 'Logan' got Ellen moving; she was secretly scared of Rose. But seconds later, while Anne was still grappling with what she'd heard, Ellen came back, still with the rolls of sheets.

'Our sheets have come up from Stores now. Logan says take these back.'

'Down to Casualty?'

'Yes, right away.' Rose Logan was walking towards them. 'I don't like the borrowing habit, so get them back at once. Yes, I do mean you, Nurse Pentrose. As for you,' she looked at Ellen, 'I want you in the side ward.' She bore Ellen off, but not before she had managed to whisper into Anne's ear:

'Now's your chance . . . go and see for yourself!'

Curiosity, and a kind of necessity, speeded Anne's steps to the lift, which swooped her down to ground level, and the entrance to Casualty. To get to Sister's office she had to walk down a centre aisle between the cubicles, most of which were empty that afternoon. She was roughly halfway through them when she heard the sound of voices, then the swishing back of one of the curtains, and Leda Hintzen herself backed out of a cubicle at the end. She hurried straight past Anne without seeing her, then a nurse appeared, then a youngish woman in a tent-like coat, carrying a child. 'Well, goodbye, Piet,' the nurse smiled at him, 'be a good brave soldier!'

'Thank goodness no lasting harm was done!' The woman set him down, he wanted to walk, and as he bent to inspect a spot on the floor, Anne got a view of his little-boy head with its cap of dark red hair, cut very close, but trying its best to curl. One of his hands was in a gauze mitten and he held it away from his body. 'Yes, it's a naughty hand, isn't it?' The woman pulled up his hood. 'He caught it in a door,' she explained, looking up and seeing Anne. 'But we're going home now, aren't we, Piet? We're just waiting for Mummy. She's gone to get her jacket, hasn't she?' The child's eyes searched her face. 'I doubt if he understands,' she said. 'He's been living in Holland. His mother wants only English spoken, so that's what I try to do.'

'Yes, of course. Excuse me.' Anne managed to get away. As Ellen had said, the woman just went on and on. And also as Ellen said, she choked, making for one of the cloakrooms, the little boy was the absolute image of Charles.

In the cloakroom, one of the staff ones, she sat down on a bench and waited for the rows of pegs, with nurses' cloaks attached, to stop turning round like a rotary linen line. Eventually they steadied, but she still sat there on the bench, trying to collect her thoughts before she went back upstairs. Piet was Charles' son . . . well, of course he was; the likeness was unmistakable. Even the eyebrows were the same—dark and level and plain. Why hadn't Leda and Charles married before Piet was born? There might be a dozen reasons why not. People very often didn't, not even when they had children, they preferred their single state. Yet Leda wanted to be married, she had made that very plain. And even if Charles no longer loved her, and who was to say he did not? he was still responsible for his own son and, being the man he was, he would never lose sight of that commitment, and he would never, because of Piet, be able to put Leda out of his life for good. He loves her all right. Anne watched a twig scraping against the window. They'll marry now, they're bound to, that's what it's all about . . . bringing the child over here to England, it's all part of their plans. Charles and Leda and Piet

belonged together as a unit, a *family unit* . . . she bit
down hard on that. What *we* had together was a fun
thing, or that's what it was to him . . . it was just for
fun, and I took it seriously.

'You look pale, Nurse. Aren't you well?' Rose Logan
enquired. She was seeing the Chaplain out of her office,
and she quickly waved him off and followed Anne
through into the ward.

'I'm fine, thank you, Staff.'

'You don't look it.' Ellen was standing by Rose. 'You
look as though you've seen a ghost, and fairly recently
too. Perhaps that one from Litchfield Cottage has
followed you all the way up here, making you look as
bloodless as Mr Lord!'

'That's enough, Nurse!' Rose's voice was sharp, so
was her glance at Anne. 'It's practically time for your
shift to end. You'd better go home and lie down. I'm
sure Nurse Tillot can cover your work for the next
twenty minutes.'

Behind her back Ellen pulled a face. Anne thanked
them both and left. She had never been so glad to be by
herself.

Charles was back on duty on Wednesday, and right on
the stroke of ten he arrived on the ward with Professor
Rawston, Susan Cleaver and four young medics. 'Got
a complete firm this morning, Sister!' the Professor
wuffed cheerfully. He led the way through the ward
doors, looking much sleeker than usual in a black suit
with a rose in his buttonhole.

'Roses in January—he must have a hothouse,' Jane
Lyne remarked. She and Anne were in Sister's office,
checking and locking away the consignment of drugs
sent up from the Pharmacy.

'Yes,' said Anne, glancing up from the ruled dispensary book. She was entering the drugs in the register,

while Jane Lyne called out the names. She was facing the big window that looked out on to the ward; she could see the doctors as they stood by the central desk. Charles rose up taller and straighter than any; he passed a hand over his head—a weary gesture over dark red hair. Anne averted her eyes:

'Dr Farne looks as though he's been through the mill . . . awful about his father.' Jane tightened the cap of a bottle and opened the drugs cupboard door.

'It's a shocking time for him, isn't it?' Anne said levelly. 'I expect he feels shattered, but he's probably glad to be able to get back to work.' He was probably glad to be back with Leda, and even the child would help . . . children often did, in terrible times, they were a kind of reassurance that life went on . . . their presence made sense of it all.

Something about the way Anne answered made Jane glance at her—not that she could see much of her face, only the smooth parted hair with its carefully pinned flotsam of cap on top. 'Well, we can't help, and that's for sure,' she said philosophically.

'I agree, we can't,' Anne replied, forcing her words through a throat that threatened to close, 'and I'm sorry, Staff, I missed that last drug you called. Was it triamterene fifty milligrammes?'

'Yes, one hundred tabs. We're just about to start the barbiturates. Use a separate page for those.' Jane called out the names, and Anne resumed writing, glad of the need to concentrate. There was always work, and she loved nursing; hadn't she vowed to herself, not so very long ago, either, that that was all she wanted? I just want to nurse, I just want to get people well, she thought.

Charles was the last to leave the ward, he had a good deal to catch up on. While Sister went to tell Tessa Merrow to make him a cup of coffee, he put his head round the office door. 'Good morning, Staff—good morning, Nurse!'

'Good morning, Doctor,' they replied in unison: they both rose to their feet.

'How have things been?'

'Oh, much the same, sir,' Jane excused herself. 'I'd better hand over these keys to Sister before I forget about them.'

'How about you, Anne?' He watched her put the dispensary book in a drawer. He went forward and stood at the desk in front of her.

'I'm well . . . please sit down. I'm sure Sister would like . . .' quickly she cleared a chair. 'I hope you're all right,' she moistened dry lips, 'I hope everything went off well. I know that's a feeble thing to say, but . . .'

'Yes, we all managed to cope.' As he sat down, as she straightened up from retrieving a pen from the floor, their eyes were level for a fleeting second; his hand touched the cuff of her dress. 'It's good to be back.'

'Work always helps.' Anne jerked away, going quickly to the door, smiling at Sister, who was entering with a tray.

'Shut the door after you, will you, please, Nurse?' Sister Grant made her way to the desk. She settled the tray, handed Charles his coffee, and watched him start to drink it. She was by no means an insensitive woman, and she wondered why it was that the atmosphere in her office seemed charged; it made her feel uncomfortable. What on earth had Dr Farne been saying to Nurse Pentrose?

Anne gave the dining-room a miss at lunchtime, and decided to walk instead—just around the hospital precinct; she felt she couldn't rest. Collecting her hat and coat from the cloakroom, she made her way downstairs, into the yard, and across to the easterly wing.

At first Charles Farne—who had just seen Leda into her blue Cortina, and watched the pole by the porters' lodge lift to let her through—didn't recognise the slender girl in the navy uniform coat and close-fitting cap, which hid most of her bright gold hair. Sometimes it seemed to him that she altered every time he saw her; he quickened his pace and managed to catch her up.

'You're not training for the Olympics, by any chance?' he joked.

'Not really, no.' She looked at him. Oh, Charles, go away, she thought. Go away and leave me in peace— why keep making overtures? Why don't you leave me alone and be as you were when I first started here— distant, disdainful, and just polite, and nothing, nothing more?

'You're not rushing off to the shops this time?'

'Nothing like that,' she said. 'I just felt like getting out on my own.'

'I think I know what you mean. The hospital atmosphere can oppress, can get one down at times.'

'Did you want anything special?' asked Anne. 'Did you call me for any reason?'

He blinked a little. Her attitude was nothing less than aggressive. Her grey-green eyes, narrowed still more against the sting of the wind, glittered and were difficult to read. Charles felt dismay, and anger too; he was unused to snubs. 'I called you for a reason, yes.' His face set as grimly as hers. 'I wanted to tell you that I called on Mrs Pentrose last evening. I was on my way back from Seftonbridge. I wanted to know how she was.'

'Oh, I see.' They turned and began to walk on, side by side, but apart. His hands were deep in his trousers' pockets, he wore no overcoat. Anne had turned her collar up, and it grazed against her face and stifled her voice, as she said at last, in slightly warmer tones: 'That was kind of you. I'm sure she was pleased. When I was home last week, she really amazed me. I thought she seemed marvellous.'

'I thought she did too. She's got good back-up help with her sister there, of course, and with Gilbertson still going in to help with the dogs at night.'

'Ray's been very good to her. He started going again, as soon as he got back from Scotland. He and Nella get on well.'

'So I gathered.' They stopped walking, and stood in the lee of a wall. Growing almost out of the bricks was a round clump of snowdrops. Charles' eyes were on the fragile blossoms, he was choosing his words with care. 'He was there last night, he took me through to see Queenie's litter.'

'He would . . . he dotes on the pups,' said Anne.

'Your grandmother tells me he's not very settled and may go back to Australia.'

'That's perfectly true. We talked about it last week when I was at home. He's not happy in England, he loathes the climate, and that I can understand.' She said this quite deliberately, giving a visible shudder and tucking her chin even deeper into her coat. They began to walk on, Anne slightly in front, and again Charles got the impression that she couldn't wait to get away from him. 'Of course,' she continued, 'he's had a rough time, he's come at the worst time of year, *and* he's been ill, which has naturally depressed him, and although he doesn't say so, I don't think he and Mr Lowe are all that compatible.'

'Mrs Pentrose thinks he'll go back to Perth.' This studied comment from Charles lay between them like a feeler, or a tacit question mark. 'She's afraid he'll persuade you to go with him.'

'It's not come to that as yet,' Anne said briskly, but

she didn't seem displeased at the notion, he thought.

'It would be natural enough, if you wanted to go back.'

'That's not what you said at first, when I first came here. You were quite scathing about people who gave things up and went off to the other side of the world.'

'I didn't know all your circumstances then.'

And now you couldn't care less, thought Anne with a twist and burst of pain. But Nella cares, of course. 'I suppose,' she said, as they reached the steps that led up to Beyton Wing, 'that Nella asked you to try to find out how settled I was here. That's unlike her, though, she usually prefers a more straightforward method. It was good of you to go and see her. I know she'd appreciate it, particularly when you must have got so much to think about, and to deal with, yourself. Thank you, it was kind.'

He looked at her for a long, long minute, his face inscrutable. The wind did its best to disturb his hair, which clung like a cap to his head—thick, dark red and exactly like the child's. A smile curved his mouth, but it didn't invite an answering smile from Anne. 'Now that,' he said, 'was a very neat way of closing the conversation, and telling me, in the nicest manner, to mind my own bloody business.'

'I didn't intend to be rude, but Ray and I will work something out. And I hope everything goes well for you. I really mean that, Charles.'

'Good wishes are always acceptable. Thank you very much. This seems to be where we part company—I'm going across to the labs.'

'Yes, of course. Goodbye,' she said. And she felt as she watched him go that this time 'goodbye' meant just that, and she'd helped to close the door. But anything was better than letting him see how she felt about him.

His real life lay with Leda and his son; there was no getting over that.

The child tied them together like husband and wife.

CHAPTER ELEVEN

'IF I had a pad like this,' said Ray, wandering from the lounge into the kitchen of Pru and Tom's flat, 'I could stick out my three years all right, even if you wouldn't share it with me!' He dropped a kiss on Anne's head. She was straightening up, tape-measure and notebook in hand.

'We're been into that before, remember?'

'Sure, yes, I know. Good friends, and all that! No wonder I'm feeling low.'

It was the third week in January. It was Saturday afternoon. Anne, at Pru's request, had come over to Martle Rise to check on two sets of window measurements that Tom had muddled up. Both Pru and Tom were on duty. 'And I *must* get that curtain material on Tuesday, Anne, so please, will you manage to go?'

Anne had been going home for the weekend, so had naturally protested. 'Ray's coming to fetch me,' she said, but at that Pru had clapped her hands.

'Well, that's perfect then, isn't it? He can run you to Martle Rise first. It's only a fifteen-minute journey, and I want you to see the flat properly, in daylight, and Ray will be interested too.'

So here they were, she and Ray, and Ray was frankly envious. 'Central heating to boot,' he said, glancing at the radiator in the little hall that gave access to all the rooms. 'You'd wonder old Tom could run to a beaut of a place like this.'

'He had a legacy when he was twenty-one—Pru told

me that. They were able to put a good sum down; their mortgage is very small.'

'I'll have to pay rent.'

'Well, don't give up. You'll find somewhere in time.' The tape-measure flicked like a snake's tongue, as Anne measured the kitchen window. She did it twice, checking it carefully, jotting the measurements down. Ray watched her from the doorway:

'I saw Farne the other night,' he said, 'around ten days ago. He called at Litchfield Cottage when I was cleaning out the dogs. He was still there when I left, making himself at home, the two old ladies were hanging on to every word he spoke.'

'I doubt if Nella was,' Anne said quietly, 'she doesn't hang on to anything. I expect she was simply glad to see him.'

'As *you* always are. I dare say if you made an effort you could get him away from the Dutch girl. She's dolly enough, but lacks your charm. I'd call her the blunderbuss type. He's attracted to you, that's fairly obvious.'

'I think you're letting your imagination run away with you, Ray.' Anne was glad he knew nothing about Leda's child, for although the gossip was rife, Ray hadn't seen Tom nor Pru during the past two weeks. They hadn't gone out in a foursome since New Year.

'She lives around here, doesn't she?' He went through to the lounge again. Anne saw him thrust back his slope of hair as he stared out of the window at the blocks of flats, all looking the same, at the streets and houses and playgrounds, at the road which ran gently downhill to the lights and the main shopping area. The road was The Rise, and gave the suburb its name. 'Whereabouts does she live?' he persisted.

'Very near here, I think. It was she who told Tom and Pru that this flat was up for sale. I rather think she's in that direction,' Anne pointed up The Rise. 'Pru ran into her last weekend, coming back this way.' She began to close the inner doors. 'I've finished, we might as well go.'

'Marriage isn't all it's cracked up to be,' Ray said moodily. 'It's all right when you first start off, but once the novelty's gone, differences show, arguments start, the differences widen like rivers, the arguments mount to full-scale rows, and love flies out of the window.'

'You married very young, you told me that. Maybe you weren't ready for it.' His outburst surprised her, even shocked her; it was unlike him to be bitter.

'I shan't get caught again,' he said, 'no marriage cage for me. Yet if, *if* . . .' the back of his hand smoothed against her cheek, 'if I'd met you first, things might have been different.'

'You can't tell that,' Anne pointed out.

'How very true.' He stepped back from her and gave her his old cheerful grin. 'In any case, I'm talking too much. You'd better blame this flat—it's giving me ideas, making me realise what I might be missing. Heigh-ho! We'd better go!' He opened the outside door. 'Do you mind if I drive around for a bit? I've got one or two things to do. I can mail that letter to my father at the post office while I'm at it. I'll pick you up in the shopping precinct, outside that hardware shop, the one called Blaxtons, with the sacks of compost out front.'

'I remember it, I'll see you there.' They took the lift to the street. Ray went to collect the car from the space at the back of the flat, while Anne began her journey down the hill.

She felt fairly certain that Ray was planning to go back to Perth. He was listing his disappointments, perhaps blaming her for some. He was gathering impetus and courage to make plans for his passage back. She felt sure of it, he wasn't hard to read. He ought to try harder, she thought, he gives up too soon. Was that why his marriage had failed? You can't cut and run from everything, she thought, then she caught herself up. How smug that sounded—as though she had the answer to every problem! And perhaps even she had cut and run when she'd come back to England, so safely with Nella, after her parents had died.

Deep in thought, she didn't notice the blue Cortina car till it slowed at the kerb and the driver pipped the horn. Startled, she turned to see Leda leaning across the seat and rolling down the nearside window. 'Hello, Anne, what a surprise! I suppose you have been to see your friend's flat?' Her wide and beautiful smile lit her face, she looked very pleased with herself. In the back, strapped into a baby-seat, sat the little boy Piet. For some reason Anne couldn't look at him, she kept her eyes fixed on Leda.

'Yes, I've been to see the flat,' she replied, 'and to do some measuring up.'

'Can I give you a lift as far as the shops, I'm on my way there now?' Leda leaned sideways and unlocked the door, but Anne quickly shook her head. 'It's nice of you, but I feel like a walk.'

Leda's eyes were amused. 'In that case I will leave you to it.' Then she looked round into the back. 'You've not met my little boy, have you? Piet, say hello to the lady. You know you can. It's the one English word he's learned so far,' she laughed.

Piet stared solemnly, his wide grey eyes, under level brows, taking stock of Anne. He wore emerald green cords and a matching jersey, a camelhair coat on top. The colours accentuated his hair, and the pink pearl of his skin. He looked at his mother, then back again at Anne.

'He's gorgeous,' said Anne, unable to stop herself

smiling in at him, in spite of the tight hand of envy and anguish and lonely hopelessness that squeezed inside her. 'He's gorgeous,' she said again.

'He is very like his father.' Leda made as if to say more, but Anne was stepping back from the car, and time was getting on, and my news can wait, Leda thought to herself, as she let in the clutch and drooled away towards the traffic lights. They changed to red just before she got there, and she slowed down and stopped. In the far distance, in her driving mirror, she could see a car approaching. She could also see Anne, who was getting close, she would soon be abreast of her. Lower down and much nearer in, she could see the top of Piet's head. She sighed. Leda was happy, things were coming right, everything was going to be all right for herself and Piet. How lucky they were!

She sat waiting at the lights.

Anne felt the rush of the Jaguar car as it ripped past her at speed, as it tore by with its drunken driver, as his bleared eyes saw the Cortina in a haze of blue, before he struck it, lifting and wrenching it round, in an instantaneous explosion of sound that split the air like a bomb, that juddered the pavement under her feet, that held her immobile in horror, before she sprang forward and covered the next few yards.

She saw nothing but Leda's car, nothing but that. Its nearside was facing her, its chassis was pointing to the middle of the road, its engine to the kerb. She saw nothing of the silver Jaguar that bounced and careered on its way, hitting a wall and bursting into flames.

She reached the Cortina, she couldn't see Leda, she saw Piet and heard his cries; then she saw the burst-open driver's door, she saw Leda on the floor, head and shoulders dangling into the road. Crowds were converging, a man was dragging Leda clear of the car. Anne scrambled inside it, and over to the back. Piet seemed to be all right, but his straps . . . his straps . . . she must get them undone, she must get him out, and fast. She smelled petrol, smelled burning, felt pain, felt terror, while the child stared fascinated at the line of flickering, greedy flames forging through the upholstery. His straps criss-crossed; Anne got them undone, and felt his astonishing weight as she pulled him forward into her arms, as she got the back door unlocked and tumbled out amidst a great shout of: *'Watch out, it's going up!'* She set the child down and ran with him; someone beat at her back; a policeman pulled them both to safety, but even from yards away she felt the whoosh and suck of the blast as the petrol tank exploded; there was a low, horrified mumble of sound from the crowd.

'The driver, where is she . . . the girl who was driving?' Anne clutched at the constable's arm.

'Over there, miss . . . there's an ambulance coming. Do you know her? Is she a friend?'

Through the legs of the crowd Anne could see Leda's hand, her arm in the pale fur coat. 'She couldn't have been wearing her safety-belt,' she said in a kind of choke. She left Piet with the policeman and made her way through to Leda. She was conscious, Anne saw her eyes move, but she was chalk-white as she tried to sit up. 'Keep as still as you can till the ambulance comes, you're going to be all right,' said Anne. 'And Piet's fine, just fine, Leda, there's nothing to worry about.'

'Want him . . . with me.' Leda scarcely seemed to move her lips as she spoke. Her hair looked dusty, lying back from her face, touching the grey pavement.

'I'll fetch him, and then you'll see. I'll come with you in the ambulance.'

'Make way . . . stand back . . . make way, please!' The stretcher was being brought through. There was a nurse with the ambulancemen, and she took charge of Piet, lifting him into the ambulance with his mother. Anne watched it pull away.

'But I wanted . . .' she began.

'You're to go in this one.' Police Constable Rivers guided her over to the second ambulance, which was easing into the kerb. There were firemen shouting orders, there were hoses all over the road, and water too, it splashed her boots, smoke and the reek of burning stained the air, making her splutter and cough.

'The other driver . . .' For the very first time she noticed the smouldering wreckage on the far side of the crossroads, humped against a wall.

'They never got him out, love,' a woman bystander said. She was chewing gum, and her jaws worked constantly, even while she spoke. 'He must have been drunk, or barmy, or bent on suicide. He seemed to me as though he tried to swerve at the very last minute. He caught the blue car right in the back, but slightly to the right. Still, you saw it, didn't you? I saw you run and get in . . . I saw you go in after that little kid.'

'I don't need an ambulance,' Anne averred. She had just remembered Ray. 'I've got to get to the hardware shop, I'm being picked up there.'

'You need hospital treatment, even if it's only a matter of first aid.' Constable Rivers was concerned about her, he knew the effects of shock, and delayed shock was sometimes the worst kind of all. He had seen Anne plunge into the car as he'd raced to the scene of the crash. He had seen the ends of her hair alight, he had beat it out with his hands, he had seen her singed sleeve, and her reddened wrist, and now he could see her trembling. 'Hospital,' he said firmly, just as Ray broke through the cordon and loped towards them, his mouth agape in a rictus of horror.

'Whatever . . . how did you . . .' It was all he could do to speak. His astonished eyes saw the scorch on Anne's coat, the ragged, singed ends of her hair, and the way she was shaking, and he snatched her to him. 'How could she have been involved?' he demanded to the constable over her head. Constable Rivers told him, as briefly as he could.

'But she needs to go to the hospital, sir, so let her get into the ambulance.'

'I've got my car, I'll follow on.' Ray watched her being helped up into the ambulance, saw a blanket go over her shoulders, saw the doors closed, and still in a daze, heard the vehicle siren away.

'It'll be the Walbrook Hospital,' Constable Rivers told him. 'Is the young lady your wife, sir?'

'I only wish she was!' Ray said thickly, going off to get his car.

The busiest time for the Accident Unit was Saturday night. When Leda and Piet and Anne were brought in at a little after four, the rush of casualties hadn't begun, and Dr Grant, Sister Grant's husband, was able to examine Leda at once. She was conscious, but dazed, and she complained of headache and intensely painful ribs. She was wheeled into X-Ray while, at her request, her friend Mrs Johns was sent for. Piet was examined and pronounced uninjured, then was put in the charge of a nurse, who kept him amused in one of the cubicles.

Anne was given hot, sweet tea, and her wrist was dressed by a staff nurse, who talked to her as though she were three years old. 'It feels sore, I'm quite sure,' she said as she laid sofra tulle over the burn, and bandaged it lightly, 'but it's superficial—a simple erythema. You were a very lucky girl indeed to have time to get out of that car.'

'She got in it to get the boy *out*, and she knew exactly

what she was risking,' Dr Grant said tartly, appearing in the cubicle entrance with his wife. Sister Grant had come down from Livingstone Ward when the news had filtered through—as it had with the speed of light, from Ellen Tillot's friend in Reception.

'Are you all right, Anne?' Josephine Grant didn't over-sympathise; she could see that Anne was right on the point of tears.

'Absolutely fine. I'll be able to go back to Block, as arranged, on Monday. I couldn't have timed it better, could I? I mean, it might have been difficult to nurse on the ward with my wrist all bandaged up.'

'I think perhaps you're going to need a few days at home, first of all. We'll find your friend Prudence Wayne; she can take you to Cade House and tuck you up for the rest of today; then tomorrow you can go home,' said Dr Grant, as they walked from the cubicle.

'Mrs Johns is here, Doctor,' an auxiliary nurse came across from Reception. 'She's come to fetch the little boy. Miss Hintzen wanted her to.'

'That's right, she did. I'll come and see her. Goodbye, Anne, and mind what I said.' He left her with Sister, who took her over to Ray in the waiting area.

'I'd like to go home Sister,' she said, as Ray sprang to his feet. 'Ray will take me, it's my weekend off, so I was going, in any case.' She didn't want to be anywhere around when Charles came in to see Leda, when Leda would tell him what had happened . . . and when he, at her request, would come over to Cade House and thank her for saving their son. I just couldn't . . . I couldn't *bear* it, she thought as she turned her face into Ray's coat. His arm tightened about her.

'Here's Pru to see you,' he said. He had seen Pru, with Tom in attendance, hurrying from the lifts. Pru was upset, almost incoherent.

'Oh, Anne, how terrible! I practically insisted on you going there, out to Martle Rise. If you hadn't gone, you wouldn't have had . . . such an awful experience! You're *frightened* of fire . . . and to go in like that, to rush into the car . . . and your hair, Anne, and your poor arm!'

'My arm's nothing, and the ends of my hair can be snipped off,' said Anne. Pru's words made her think, perhaps think too much, because if she hadn't been there, if she hadn't gone to Martle Rise, Leda wouldn't have seen her, she wouldn't have stopped to offer her a lift, and if she hadn't stopped she would have caught the lights at green, and gone smoothly and safely over.

'It was a mercy the driver of that Jag didn't plough through a dozen people,' said Ray, then added, 'poor devil!' and squeezed Anne's hand very tight. 'I'm taking Anne home,' he told Pru and Tom, and the grave-faced Sister Grant. 'Mrs Pentrose's doctor will decide when she's fit to come back.' Perhaps for the first time ever Ray took charge of a situation and handled it firmly, making his meaning plain.

Dr Grant returned to tell them that Leda's condition wasn't serious. 'Her films show no bony injury, but we're keeping her in for the present. She has slight concussion and severe bruising, consistent, I would think, with having been thrown against her door; she wasn't wearing her belt—says she forgot it,' he jerked his chin in the air. 'As for you, Anne, I'll give you a set of dressings for that wrist. It'll want re-doing each morning, but Mrs Pentrose will cope with that. Once a nurse, always a nurse . . . at least, so they say.' They all laughed in a forced kind of manner; talking was proving a strain. Anne was thankful when she and Ray were on their way at last, driving through the traffic towards Mill Hill.

Darkness had closed in quickly, and the glare of headlamps and lights hurt her eyes. 'Are you all right, Annie?' Ray heard her shift in her seat.

'Yes, I'm all right.'

'Does your arm hurt?'

'Not really, just stings a bit.' She looked at him. 'It's all right, Ray, you *can* talk , you know, there's no need to sound so wary. I'm not in a state of shock.' She laughed as she spoke, pushing back the nausea which threatened to encroach, along with a vision of Leda's blazing car. At the time it had happened she'd been frightened, but fully able to cope. She'd had Piet to think about, of course, and then there had been Leda, lying there, looking so ghastly ill. How strange it was that in retrospect it seemed closer and even more real. She welcomed the sound of Ray's voice . . . just keep talking, she thought, keep talking and talking, I don't care what about.

'I didn't know the Dutch girl had a child,' he was saying.

'Well, she does.'

'Is it Farne's?'

'People say so.'

'Do *you* believe it is?'

'Perhaps . . . I don't know . . . well, yes, I do.' Anne could hear her voice going up.

'You saved its life,' Ray reminded her.

'*It* is a he, and if I hadn't saved him, someone else would have. Goodness knows, there were plenty of people about.'

'But not all prepared to do what you did. That policeman said you were quick—he said he'd never seen anything like it. Hintzen and Farne will be grateful—undyingly grateful.' The faintest of sneers tinged his voice.

'I don't want their gratitude, that's the last thing I want. I'd have done the same for anyone . . . anyone's child, or I hope I would. I'd do the same again, as my parents . . . my parents did!' Anne broke off in distress, and began to cry, then found she couldn't stop.

Ray pulled into a side road and drew her against his shoulder; her hair smelled of smoke, it felt stiff and spiny. His voice was rough in her ear. 'Come back with me, Anne . . . come home with me, back to Australia. That's where you belong, we both belong there, you know you're not happy here. Leave it, leave it all behind, start afresh in Perth. You could nurse there, train there. Please come . . . oh, please, please come!'

His words cut through to her, halted her crying. His arms were comforting, his face was warm, and perhaps for a second—for a second, two seconds, three— perhaps she was tempted, perhaps she wavered, perhaps she thought, oh yes, yes, yes, get away, I'll leave it all behind. But the seconds ticked on, they flew on their way, little specks of madness, trying to make her take a mistaken course. 'No, Ray, I belong here.' She sat up and blew her nose. 'It's only just lately, when things have gone wrong, that I've got a little restive.'

'If I asked you to marry me, would you come then?'

'No, not even then, but you aren't going to ask me to marry you, you don't believe in marriage. You're pulling out all the stops now because you see me like this, upset and everything, and you mind about me, and that's human and . . . and very nice.' She smiled at him and put her hand over his. 'You see, I know the feeling. I've had it for you, it comes in flashes, but I had it most of all when you were ill and, to some extent, were dependent on me in hospital. I had it that day you hurt your arm—then most especially. It's a sort of caring, but it's not the kind that goes on for ever and ever. You don't want to marry me, Ray, any more than I do you . . . not really, not deep down, not in . . . not in cold blood.'

'That's a droll way of putting it!' His heart beat painfully. Yet her words held a ring of truth, and he knew it; he stared out over the wheel. A woman was crossing the road with a dog—some sort of white poodle, a girl cycled by, and her rear light was a speck in the distance before he collected himself enough to switch the ignition on and say with a kind of false heartiness: 'At least we've cleared the air. I intend to go back, nothing alters that, but I'm going to miss you, Anne.'

'I'll miss you,' she said quietly; he could feel her looking at him. Surprising himself, he turned and kissed her brow.

'I hope things aren't so bad that we can't be friends for the time I've got left.' The broad grin she was so used to seeing spread across his face. 'You see, I don't want to have to stop coming along to the Cottage. You know how attached I am to Queenie's pups!'

He had struck the right note. 'In that case, feel free. Of course we're friends,' she said. She tried to laugh, but felt so tired that even to move her lips felt as though she were straining on heavy weights. Seeing the way she slumped in her seat, Ray turned the car for home. Half an hour later they were driving down West Farm Lane.

CHAPTER TWELVE

NELLA was looking out for them. Pru had rung her up and told her what had happened, so she knew what to expect. Even so, the sight of Anne's face as Ray brought her into the cottage appalled her; she got her to bed at once.

Great-Aunt Flo, her sister, didn't help very much. 'I think you should send for the doctor, Nella; she looks very ill to me. I think she ought to have stayed at the hospital.'

'A good night's rest will work wonders,' Nella sounded cross. 'If she isn't considerably better by the morning, then of *course* I'll send for the doctor.'

Aunt Flo subsided, and went out to heat up some soup.

Jolly found his way upstairs, he thought it was his duty to accompany his young mistress at such a time. He wasn't a dog for sleeping on beds, so Nella brought up his bean-bag. He settled himself, not making a sound, just going downstairs once to be let out into the garden at half-past ten.

Anne heard him come upstairs again, then she heard Nella and Aunt Flo bolting doors and slipping on chains and switching off the lights. She heard Aunt Flo mounting the stairs, trying to be quiet, she heard Nella's stick as she entered her bedroom downstairs.

After that there were only the night sounds—the hum of traffic far off, a dog barking—not one of theirs—the bray of a diesel train as it hurtled its way to St Albans and the North.

Two scenes played out in her head, spun through like a reel of film—first the scene with Leda when she had offered her a lift, then the one where she had lain on the pavement after the accident, asking for Piet, with her bright hair in the dust. Would Charles know about the accident? Would someone have rung him up? Susan had told her he was going home to Seftonbridge for the weekend. Someone would have let him know, he would go straight off to see Leda. All I hope is he doesn't come here, feeling he's got to thank me, thought Anne. She hunched herself up and thumped at her pillow; even that reeked of smoke. First thing tomorrow she would wash her hair and get Nella to cut off the ends.

Jolly turned round on his bean-bag. Anne did her best to sleep. Outside the wind was veering north-east, blowing sleet across the fields. The English winter was nowhere near done. I can't wait to get out of it, Ray Gilbertson thought, lying sleepless three miles away.

'There've been several calls from London already,' Nella told Anne next morning.

It was ten o'clock. 'I'm ashamed of myself for having slept so long.' Anne drank some coffee, and reached for the toast. Aunt Flo had gone to church, and Nella and Anne were breakfasting on their own. 'Who were the calls from, Nella? I expect Pru was the first.'

'She was, yes, then Dr Cleaver, and then, believe it or not, Sister Tutor, ringing from her home.'

'Whatever for?' asked Anne, astonished.

'To tell you to stay at home until mid-week. You're due back in Block, she told me.'

'Mm, for the whole of next week.'

'It'll just be for half a week now. She says you'll soon catch up. Everyone seems very concerned. You've made your mark at the Walbrook,' remarked Nella. 'Any time now I expect we'll be having a call from Charles Farne.

After all, you saved his girl-friend's son. I would have thought *she* ought to have rung.'

'She probably doesn't feel up to it,' said Anne.

'I didn't take to her much. I used to see her in Anderson Ward, when I was laid up with my leg. She tried to get me to start some tapestry, but I soon told her no. If Charles marries her he'll rue it, but he's just the sort of man to fall for a hard-luck story. How old is her little boy?'

'Eighteen months, or two years, I should think.' Anne buttered a slice of toast. It plainly hadn't occurred to Nella that Charles might be the father. Not wanting to further the conversation, she changed it deliberately, telling her grandmother that Ray was returning to Perth. 'He wanted me to go with him, but I told him no, I couldn't. I like it here. I intend to make my plans work.'

Her words fell on Nella's ears like music, her relief was absolute. 'Good,' was all she managed to say, but the single expletive spoke volumes, so did the look she gave Anne. 'For goodness' sake,' she cried, 'we'll have to do something about your hair! What a *mess* you look!' Then the phone rang again, and this time it was Charles.

Anne sat down on the hall chair, holding the phone to her face; he was saying that he had only just heard, and was she really all right?

'Perfectly all right, absolutely fine,' she said with a little laugh.

'You're sure?'

'Of course. How's Leda?'

'Shaky, so Susan Cleaver said—it was Susan who telephoned me. Anne, I'd like to see you. I'm starting back for Town now. May I call in at the Cottage on the way?'

'Of course you can, we'll be pleased to see you.' Her

words were ones of welcome, but her tone was flat and completely lacking in warmth.

'I'll be with you at around twelve or half-past. Goodbye until then.' He rung off, and Anne went to tell Nella the news.

'I knew he would come. I'd have thought it very strange indeed if he didn't,' said Nella in a clipped sort of voice, moving Jolly off her lap. 'If he's coming at midday, then he might as well stay to lunch. It'll set him up for the rest of his journey to Town.'

It was nearly one o'clock when Charles' Mercedes nosed up the drive, through a thin fine snow blowing sideways like a veil. By then Anne's hair, snipped three inches shorter, swung in a bell to her shoulders. Her sweater was scarlet, her kilt a tartan; she felt brilliance was necessary. It would lend a kind of spurious courage, which she knew she was going to need. Charles might easily be going to tell her all about his child, and about his impending marriage perhaps, for the shock of the accident might have made him realise how much Leda meant to him. The car stopped and the driver's door opened wide.

'I'll let him in,' said Nella, 'you stay here by the fire. I'll keep Flo out of the way too, you don't want her chipping in.' Moving quite well for an elderly lady with a recently mended leg, she reached the front door just as Charles pressed his thumb on the bell.

Anne stood up, then sat again, agitation outweighing poise. Minutes passed . . . why didn't he come? Nella was keeping him, she could hear their voices murmuring in the hall. She pressed her hands together, jumping to her feet as the door opened and shut, and there he was. 'Hello, how are you?' He noted her pallor, her new length of hair, the white bandage under the scarlet cuff.

'Perfectly all right, as I told you. Sit down, Charles, and get warm.'

Anne had to sit down rather quickly herself, or her legs might have given way. He seated himself in the easy chair opposite. He was facing the light, she could see him clearly . . . every hair, every line, every crinkle. He sat forward, his hands between his knees, and his eyes moved over her face in the way she remembered; she began to tremble again. 'I once told you you were brave,' he said, 'now you've proved my words to be true.'

'It was impulse more than bravery. I acted and thought later. I have a habit of doing that.' They laughed a little uncomfortably. Neither felt happy, there was unease in the room.

'How is your wrist?' asked Charles.

'Quite bearable. When it happened I didn't feel it. It must have been when I was lifting Piet out; the flames were on his right side.'

'And your hair?' His voice rasped.

'Caught in flight! Serves me right for wearing it loose. As it is now I'll probably find I can keep my cap on better.'

'It suits you.' He looked away and beyond her to the window. 'It's an awful morning.' .

'I know it is. You really shouldn't have stopped.'

'Your grandmother asked me to lunch, and I'm staying.' Charles held his hands out to the fire. 'She has also just whispered in my ear that you're staying here in England, that you're not going back to Perth with Gilbertson.'

'She's pleased about it. She's apt to think that every-one else will be too,' Anne told him.

'Did he ask you to marry him?'

'As an afterthought, yes, but it wasn't what he

wanted. I didn't . . . don't want . . . any of it. All I really want is to stay in London and further my career.' Put like that it sounded pompous. She expected him to laugh, but he didn't, he got up and paced the room, and in turning to follow his movements Anne bumped her wrist on the arm of her chair and was quite unable to stop a sharp exclamation bursting out of her throat. Charles was with her in seconds.

'Oh, Anne . . . oh, Anne, Anne, my very dear!' He drew her up out of the chair, holding her carefully, as though she might break, kissing her cheeks and hair. She wrenched herself free, her wrist stung and throbbed, and tears of pain-driven anger made her snap at him and forget to guard her tongue.

'Save your endearments for Leda and your son! Why can't you leave me alone? Are you so vain that . . .' And then she stopped as she saw the look on his face.

'I'm not vain at all, and Piet's not my son!' he said angrily.

'Not . . .' She stared at him.

'He's my brother's child, Mark's child.' Still Anne stared blank-faced.

'Surely you remember me telling you about my brother in Johannesburg?' He moved away and went to the window again.

'I do now,' her voice was quiet. 'You told me about him that evening when you drove me home after the party at Professor Rawston's house. I don't know how I could have forgotten, but even if I'd remembered, I don't suppose, I doubt if I would have . . . would ever have connected the two.'

'You connected me!'

'You and Leda were always together,' she pointed out.

'It looked that way, I dare say.' He came back and

stood with her; each searched the other's face. 'I think explanations are due.'

'Charles, you don't have to.' And she meant that, he didn't have to explain, he didn't have to . . . all she wanted was to take in what he had said. Piet wasn't his, so perhaps . . . perhaps . . .

'I want to tell you,' he said. 'Please hear me out, I need to tell you, and then you can judge me, Anne. It wasn't my story to tell before, it belonged entirely to Leda, and it all began three years ago when I went to Amsterdam to see Mark, who was working there at that time.' He sat down, so did she. The chair seemed to receive her and hold her fast as she listened to his words. 'It was a bad time for me,' Charles continued. 'I'd just been walked out on by a girl who meant a very great deal to me. Mark and Leda were living together, were fathoms deep in love. Leda was working, enjoying her job, everything was right. I envied them, envied their happiness, and I went back to Seftonbridge feeling, I think, that life was passing me by. Three months later Mark wrote to say he was being transferred to Johannesburg. He came home to say goodbye—I was working at Seftonbridge then— and when I asked about Leda he said the affair was finished, with no hard feelings on either side. I was surprised, but thought no more about it till I got a letter from Leda, asking me if I would give her Mark's address. She was pregnant, she said . . . she must have his address. I didn't give it at first. I telephoned Mark in Johannesburg, who showed very little interest, and no concern, he said the child might not be his. I didn't believe him, and said so; he laughed at me over the phone. He said if I were so concerned I'd better take Leda on. "Let her run *you* into a corner"—I can hear him saying it now. I went over to Amsterdam the next weekend.

'I had a stony reception from Leda's family . . . she was living back at home by then. I gave her Mark's address, but he disclaimed all responsibility. I felt I had to do something, I thought a lot of Leda, so I helped her financially over that time. When Piet was six months old I went to Amsterdam to see him. There was no doubt he was Mark's son, the family likeness was strong. When I wrote to Mark I stressed this, but he simply ignored the whole thing. Leda said she didn't care; she had got her old job back; she didn't, she said, need any more help from me.

'Not long after I got my present post at the Walbrook, Leda wrote to me again. She sent some photographs of Piet, she thought I might like to see them. We began to write on a regular basis, and that summer she came to London. She told me she wanted to work in England, she had friends there, she said, and as you know . . .' Charles' tone altered slightly as he looked directly to Anne, 'she spoke English practically perfectly.'

'Yes, she did . . . *does*, I mean,' Anne agreed quietly. Charles had nothing but praise for Leda, he upheld her all the time. He must be in love with her, so why was he saying all this? She looked away from his face to her hands, then moved them in her lap; they didn't seem to be joined to her at all.

'As it happened I was able to help her,' he said after a pause. 'Not that she didn't get the job at the Walbrook on her own merits . . . she did, she was the best of the applicants. Piet had to be left in Holland, but Leda's idea was to find living quarters of a kind that would mean she could have him with her. She adored him. She went home every month.'

'She's a strong character,' Anne suggested.

'She is, she's very determined. I admired her pluck, I enjoyed her company, and we had fun . . . a lot of laughs. I knew people gossiped about us, but that didn't worry me. It was only when I realised that Leda was laying false trails, deliberately leading people to think our liaison was serious, that I began to feel, to quote my brother, that she was running me into a corner, looking for a father for her son. And just to keep the record straight, there was no grand passion between us. She had been Mark's girl, she had had his child; to me that made a barrier, one that I didn't even want to climb.

'We had it out on Christmas Eve—a fine time to choose! I said I thought we ought not to pair up quite so frequently. Leda said "Okay", in that way she has. I don't think she cared over-much. She was full to the brim with her new flat, and with getting Piet over from Holland. Perhaps she was even tired of lying —because that was what she'd been doing. "Well, at least you can come and see your nephew," was the last thing she said. And I had to laugh; that was typical Leda— oh, so *typical* Leda! She absolutely refuses to be squashed.'

'She does . . . yes.' Anne could hardly breathe. It was finished, all finished between them. Charles wasn't in love with Leda . . . she had just dazzled him, that was all. He had enjoyed playing Sir Galahad.

'When Father died, Mark came home,' he continued quietly. 'I was determined that he and Leda should meet. Mark knew she was at the Walbrook, I'd mentioned that in my letters. What he didn't know was that when I invited him to dine in Medical Residents', I had also invited Leda, and told her Mark would be there. She didn't bat an eyelid, she took it all in her stride; she dressed herself up and swanned in, and if Mark wasn't overjoyed, he was at any rate un-angered, and more than intrigued, especially when—with masterly timing—Leda showed him a snapshot of Piet. He asked to see him, Leda agreed, and he went home with her that night. Since then I know they've been seeing one another. Mark is here for several weeks, working at his head office in the Strand.'

'It's just like a story!' Anne got her breath back. 'Will they marry, do you think?'

'I don't know, it's too soon to say, but I think they'll get back together. Mark was at the hospital with Leda all last evening. He was sent for by Mrs Johns—he was staying with friends at the Barbican. He, too, rang me this morning. He's very anxious to meet you. He wants to thank you—so does Leda.'

'There's no need for that,' shrugged Anne.

A peremptory bark sounded out in the hall, and Anne let Jolly in. He wagged himself over to sit by the fire, and Charles shot up out of his chair, intercepting Anne as she returned. 'There's need for me to make something clear.' He took her hands in his, holding them down at her sides as though he thought she might try to escape. 'The girl I was once engaged to was a doctor at Seftonbridge General. She threw everything up, including me, to emigrate to Australia. When she went I was stricken,' his eyes held Anne's, 'and it took me an age to recover; I felt I hated the very sound of the word Australia. Three years later you appeared, and I felt it was going to happen all over again, only much more painfully. I felt the gods were laughing themselves sick at my expense. You see, I fell in love with you practically at first sight . . . certainly from the night of the party, and I kept going deeper in, helplessly, hopelessly, crazily, deeper and deeper in love with you. That night we spent here at Litchfield Cottage—together, but apart—I'll never know how I managed not to tell you how I felt. I was so sure it was Ray you wanted, Ray Gilbertson, who could take you home to Australia and give you your old life back.'

Anne shook her head.

'What does that mean?' Charles drew her into his arms.

'It means,' she said, with her cheek against his, 'that I don't love Ray like that, that I don't want my old life back, that my home is here in England. And more than any of those things, more than anything else, it means that I love you with all my heart, and have done since the party, when you brought me home and listened to me, and I knew you understood.'

'And I kissed you and felt the world explode.'

'A kind of shattering.'

'Exactly that.' His eyes were tender. 'Oh, Anne, my dearest girl, let's get married very soon, don't keep me waiting long.'

She took his face between her hands, loving the feel of his skin, hard-soft, smooth-rough . . . she traced the line of his chin. There was confidence now, joy now, an elation born of the knowledge that all she felt he was feeling too . . . it was like a miracle.

Charles bent and kissed her, holding her fast, her body merged with his, and along with the rush of sweetness, the curl of ecstasy, was a deep-seated, deeply-felt sense of security, which would hold them together through all the problems of life.

They were married from Litchfield Cottage, much to Nella's delight, in the little church at Windon, on a mad March day—a day of strong winds to lift the veil of the beautiful young bride, but a day of brilliant sunshine too, to shine on the happy couple, on the milling crowd of relatives and friends.

Grandfather Lingate, all the way from Canberra, gave

Anne away. Mark was best man, and Pru, only two weeks married herself, was matron of honour. Ray sent a cable from Perth.

Back at the Cottage, during the reception, Nella answered a host of questions. 'Yes, Anne intends to complete her training,' she told a cousin from Rhyl. 'Charles and she will live in the doctors' married quarters till June, and after that they'll move to the house they're buying at Hampstead. No, I don't know when they'll start a family, that's rather a personal question.

'Really,' she said, moving across to speak to Charles' mother, 'the questions one gets asked, Elizabeth . . . no reticence at all!' Then she listened with pleasure to Elizabeth's news, which concerned Mark and Leda. They were being married quietly in London in three weeks' time, after which, with their son Piet, they would fly out to Johannesburg. 'Good,' said Nella, in the forthright way she had.

While innumerable objects were being attached to the Mercedes in the driveway, she went upstairs to help Anne out of her dress. And this, she thought, as she crossed the landing, is one of the happiest occasions, if not *the* happiest occasion, to ever grace that house.

And it might have been the champagne she had drunk, for she never drunk much as a rule, but she was absolutely certain, as she turned the knob of Anne's door, that she could hear faintly, somewhere far off, but somewhere in the house . . .

The silvery, tinkling notes of a harpsichord.

Mills & Boon

4 Doctor Nurse Romances
FREE

Coping with the daily tragedies and ordeals of a busy hospital, and sharing the satisfaction of a difficult job well done, people find themselves unexpectedly drawn together. Mills & Boon Doctor Nurse Romances capture perfectly the excitement, the intrigue and the emotions of modern medicine, that so often lead to overwhelming and blissful love. By becoming a regular reader of Mills & Boon Doctor Nurse Romances you can enjoy SIX superb new titles every two months plus a whole range of special benefits: your very own personal membership card, a free newsletter packed with recipes, competitions, bargain book offers, plus big cash savings.

**AND an Introductory FREE GIFT for YOU.
Turn over the page for details.**

**Fill in and send this coupon back today
and we'll send you**

4 Introductory
Doctor Nurse Romances yours to keep
FREE

At the same time we will reserve a
subscription to Mills & Boon
Doctor Nurse Romances for you. Every
two months you will receive the latest
6 new titles, delivered direct to your door.
You don't pay extra for delivery. Postage and
packing is always completely Free.
There is no obligation or commitment –
you receive books only for
as long as you want to.

It's easy! Fill in the coupon below and return it to
**MILLS & BOON READER SERVICE, FREEPOST, P.O. BOX 236,
CROYDON, SURREY CR9 9EL.**

Please note: **READERS IN SOUTH AFRICA** write to
**Mills & Boon Ltd., Postbag X3010,
Randburg 2125, S. Africa.**

- -

FREE BOOKS CERTIFICATE

**To: Mills & Boon Reader Service, FREEPOST, P.O. Box 236,
Croydon, Surrey CR9 9EL.**

Please send me, free and without obligation, four Dr. Nurse Romances, and reserve a Reader
Service Subscription for me. If I decide to subscribe I shall receive, following my free parcel of
books, six new Dr. Nurse Romances every two months for £6.00 , post and packing free. If I
decide not to subscribe, I shall write to you within 10 days. The free books are mine to keep in
any case. I understand that I may cancel my subscription at any time simply by writing to you. I
am over 18 years of age.
Please write in BLOCK CAPITALS.

Name _____

Address _____

_____

_____

_____ Postcode _____

SEND NO MONEY — TAKE NO RISKS

EP1